CatchMe

If You Can

FRIENDS FOREVER 1

ANITA DAVIS

ISBN-10: 1-946721-02-6
ISBN-13: 978-1-946721-02-0

Books may be purchased in quantity by contacting the author Anita Davis:
Set Apart Publishing
PO Box 39229
Chicago, IL 60659
or by email at authoranitadavis@gmail.com

ACKNOWLEDGEMENTS

I want to thank God and my couch for helping me write this book.

I owe my gratitude to the authors I met via book festivals and in my online writing course that gave me suggestions to help me with different strategies in writing this story and their willingness to share their triumphs and tragedies with their works. I'm definitely able and willing to glean from them.

Special, special thanks to Mom, my friends Crystal Alexis, and Keleigh Creiger Hadley, my cousin Michelle. and sorority sister Trease who listened to my concerns with writing this and gave me their honest feedback and consistent encouragement to finish it. Thank you ladies so much.

My sister/friend Gabrielle Marcell rocks. She knows exactly what she did to help me with publishing this book and I thank her so much for everything.

Thank you to anyone else who helped but I may have not mentioned by name.

ENJOY

The course of true love never did run smooth.

William Shakespeare

1

"Seems like you've been running all your life. When are you going to slow down?" Melanie Daniels asked her best friend, Karen.

"When you run, you get to where you want to go faster." Karen Roberts laughed as she tied her gym shoes.

"Well, where exactly are you trying to get to because it ain't to a man?" Melanie retorted as she begrudgingly tied her running shoes. "Why am I running with you again? On Lake Shore Drive? At this time of the morning?"

Karen put out her hand to number her answers per finger. "I'm not running to or from a man. You know, whether it's on a trail with my sneakers or across the city or even the country, I run because there's so much that I want to accomplish in life. Um, what else?"

Melanie bore a pinched expression as she listened to Karen's rant.

Karen ignored Melanie's annoyed look and continued, "Oh, you run with me because you love the way you look in your running shorts during the

1

summer. And we run on Lake Shore Drive really early in the morning because at the end of our run we get to watch the beautiful sun rise against Lake Michigan. And oh yea, going as early as we do, we get out there before all the other runners do. I just like it to be me and the pavement."

"Well, since you like it that way, let me just go back over to my apartment and get back in bed then." Melanie turned to walk out the door.

"You will not. Come on, let's go." Karen pulled Melanie out of the door and to the elevator before Melanie was tempted to go back to her own apartment across the hall.

***

Kyle Irving still couldn't believe that his team lost in the NBA finals in game seven. They had fought hard to make a comeback being down three games to win three straight.

Coming so close to his dream then not achieving it was too much for him to handle. He left Miami immediately after the game hoping to escape the media and the embarrassment of not winning. He needed to go somewhere quiet and think about his trade options. He would be nearing the end of his pro-basketball career in a few more years, and he still didn't have what every player dreamed of—a championship ring.

He stayed in Hawaii for a week before he decided to return to his hometown, Chicago.

He had bought his parents a nice home out in

Oakbrook Terrace, so he knew he could visit them there if he wanted, but he didn't have to since he had a condo downtown on north Lake Shore Drive.

In addition to his already impressive career, Kyle knew that he needed to be in the best shape if he planned on being picked up by a championship contending team. Running was a way he stayed in shape. He loved to run, and he loved to do it along Lake Shore Drive early in the morning before it would be filled with runners and cyclists. It was something about the wind hitting his face as he ran that calmed him and helped to escape the crazy reality of his celebrity lifestyle.

Kyle left out of his apartment in search of serenity along his run.

***

"I swear I love to run, I just hate doing it so early in the morning. It's dark out here. Where are you, Mr. Sun?" Melanie slowed her pace and extended her open arms to the dark skies.

Karen shuffled backward in front of Melanie. "He's waiting on you to stop complaining and get ready to embrace him."

"Karen, watch out," Melanie called out.

"Hunh?" Karen almost did a backward flip over a man kneeling to tie his shoes, but somehow he managed to catch her before she hit the ground.

He took his headphones out. "Are you okay?" He placed her back on her feet.

"Yes, I'm okay. I'm so sorry for bumping into

you like that." Karen allowed one hand to keep its grip on his firm bicep and used the other to pat her short pixie hairdo to make sure it was still intact.

They were so close that she could feel his washboard abs contract up against her breasts as he breathed.

She closed her eyes for a second, taking in the sporty scent of his cologne. She exhaled deeply and opened her eyes again.

He let go of her when he realized she had fully regained her balance. Kyle lost himself in her dark brown eyes. He smiled inwardly at how her long eyelashes looked as if they were tickling her eyelid from all the blinking that she was doing.

Melanie ran closer to them. "You okay, girl?" She looked at Kyle. "Hi, I'm Melanie and this here helpless pup is Karen."

Karen worked hard to pull her attention away from Kyle's full lips. They looked so kissable. She shot a skeptical look at Melanie. She returned her gaze back to the dark caramel, handsome man and was grateful that her mocha skin hid her blushing cheeks.

He smirked. "Hi Melanie. Hi Karen. I'm Kyle."

Karen quivered from the bass in his voice.

"So, Kyle, we've never seen you out here before. What brings you out here so early in the morning?" Melanie asked since Karen couldn't seem to find her voice.

Kyle stared at Karen. "I like running early in the morning before anyone else is out here. Just me and my thoughts. It's also good conditioning for what I do."

"Oh really?" Melanie nudged Karen with her elbow.

Karen cleared her throat. Her perfectly arched eyebrows lifted. "So, what is it that you do, Kyle?"

He loved to hear her speak. Her smoky voice captivated him.

"I'm a professional basketball player."

"You mean NBA professional basketball type of player?" Karen stepped back from him with a snarl on her lips and the sudden recognition of who he was.

"Yes," Kyle spoke slowly noting Karen's sudden change in her mood.

Melanie noticed Karen's deflated mood as well.

"Karen, I hope I'm not being too forward, and I know we just met, but can I take you out sometime? I want to get to know you more." Kyle wasn't used to women backing off from him like she seemed to be doing, so he didn't know what to do with himself standing there waiting for her response. He normally would be storing the woman's number in his phone at that point.

The sun was rising. The vibrant hues of yellow and orange melted the darkness of the skies as it kissed the water.

Karen averted eye contact with him. "Sorry, I can't. I'm taken. Come on, Melanie, let's go."

Karen and Melanie took off running again.

The beautiful backdrop of the sun rising should have served as the perfect scenery to start Kyle and Karen's romance. Instead, Kyle stood under it alone, wondering how he had held Karen's attention with his eyes one moment and in the very next, she wouldn't even look into them.

"Girl slow down." Melanie drew in deep breaths trying to slow her heart rate down. "I want to know why you just lied to that fine man saying that you're taken. By who, and why haven't I met him?"

"Whatever." Karen kept looking ahead.

"Why didn't you take Kyle up on his offer for a date? You couldn't stop gawking at him, barely said two words to him, so I know you like him."

Karen picked up her pace.

"Stop." Melanie pulled on Karen's arm with enough force to stop their run. "What's up? You talk about wanting a great man to pursue you, but whenever they try, you shoot them down. You just had an NBA player gawk at you and ask you out, and you turn him down. Why?"

"That's exactly why I turned him down. He's an NBA player. That means a horrible reputation with women precedes him." Karen took off running again.

2

"Karen, look ahead," Melanie shouted.

"Hunh?" Karen asked, confusion marring her forehead.

"Look who's sitting on that bench ahead of us." Melanie motioned her head forward.

"Ugh, is that him from yesterday?"

"Haaa. Don't act like you don't know his name, especially since you couldn't stop talking about him all last night." Melanie chided Karen.

"Whatever."

"Don't whatever me. Clearly, you're attracted to the man. Just give him a chance," Melanie pleaded.

"Nope." Karen sprinted faster ahead of Melanie and right past Kyle.

Kyle jumped up from the bench and ran in stride with Melanie.

"So, what's up with your girl?"

"What do you mean?"

"How she was yesterday. One minute we're staring each other down with admiration, and the next minute, she looks at me with disgust and then runs off from me."

"It's girl code. I can't tell you." Melanie laughed.

"Girl code?"

"Yeah, girl code. You know, y'all have it too."

Kyle laughed inwardly knowing that there was a "guy code", but he would never let a woman in on it.

Melanie continued, "You all don't share each other's secrets with us. You leave us clueless not knowing what goes on in your heads. Well, I'm doing the same. You're going to have to ask her if you really want to know."

"I'll try."

Kyle eyed Karen's petite yet curvy frame from behind before he ran faster to catch up with her. He ran alongside her. "Hey, Karen."

"Who run the world? Girls. Who run the world? Girls…" Karen sang the Beyonce song as loud as she could feigning not being able to hear Kyle speak.

"Karen. Hey, Karen." He waved, now running backward in front of her.

"Oh, hey," she said flatly trying to mask her attraction to him. She took her headphones out.

"How are you?" he asked.

"Good, just trying to finish my run strong." She proceeded to put her headphones back in, but he spoke to her again.

"I knew you seemed familiar yesterday. You're a sportscaster for ESPN, aren't you?" Kyle asked.

"Yes, I am." She continued to look straight ahead as Kyle repositioned himself running next to her.

"I guess I just didn't notice you right away. You weren't in your business clothes." Kyle shook his head at himself, thinking on how lame he must have sounded to Karen. He was fishing for anything to say to her to keep the conversation going.

I wish he would just stop talking to me already. Why does he have to be so handsome? "Yeah, I guess I do look unrecognizable when I'm not all glammed up for the camera."

"Naw, you're very beautiful without the makeup. With sweat dripping from your forehead. With your moments of ignoring me as we run right now." Kyle laughed.

"Thanks. Not ignoring you, I just thought we both shared yesterday that we like to run in the morning to avoid other runners and just focus on our thoughts and the pavement. How can I, we, do that if you continue to talk to me now?" Karen looked back to see Melanie keeping a suspicious running distance from them.

"Feisty, aren't you?" Kyle laughed again.

"I didn't recognize you at first yesterday because you seem so much taller on the basketball court, but it hit me after a while who you were, especially after admitting you play pro-ball."

"Ouch." Kyle shook his head.

Although he would have taken that as a low blow from someone else, it was cute when she said it. He knew he would relish in getting to know her.

"Since you like being so blunt I guess I can, too. I like you, Karen. I'm trying to get to know you, but it seems as if you keep blowing me off. Why?"

Karen furrowed her eyebrows. "I try not to judge, but you're an NBA player. With all of the locker room chats, interviews, and expose's I've done over the years, I know exactly how you all can be when it comes to women."

"Oh really? And how is that?"

"Man-whores."

"Haaa! What?"

"You heard me. Man whores. Love 'em and leave 'em, frequent booty calls, married and cheating, several baby mommas, I can go on and on." Karen pulled her water bottle from her waist belt and took a sip.

Kyle couldn't help but to stare at her plump lips as they puckered around the water bottle opening. He cleared his throat and wiped sweat from dripping into his eyes. "You are something else." He laughed. "I get why you would think I'm like that, but trust me, I'm not."

"That's what you say."

"That's what I know."

"So you've never done any of the things that I mentioned?"

Kyle frowned. "Yes, but..."

"Like I said, man-whores." Karen broke eye contact with him and sprinted off as fast as she could.

Kyle stopped and leaned on a nearby rail. Melanie caught up to him. He spoke through wispy breaths. "Do you think I have a chance with her?"

"I don't know. It depends on how bad you want her."

3

Karen lowered herself until her forehead touched her knees. She stayed that way for fifteen seconds before switching to another stretching position.

Melanie tightened her shoe strings as she sat and leaned forward to stretch her hamstrings. "So no talk of him last night I see."

"Nope. I'm not even going to waste another moment talking or thinking about him. I just want to enjoy my silent run this morning."

"And that's exactly what you'll get if he doesn't catch up with you."

"What?"

"I'm not even taking our regular route this morning. I have a gnawing feeling that if I do, I'll just end up running by myself again, so I'll do myself a favor and go the opposite way." Melanie smirked.

"Nooooo. Don't do that. Run with me, please." Karen gripped Melanie's shoulders.

"Nope. Won't do it. And if you look ahead, you'll see why I'm running this way." Melanie took off running in the opposite direction of their normal route.

Karen turned around to see Kyle running toward her.

She took off running in Melanie's direction.

"Karen. Wait up."

"Hunh? I can't hear you."

"I said wait up." Kyle huffed and ran faster to catch up with Karen.

She picked up her pace.

"Karen."

Music blared in Karen's ears as she ran away smiling.

***

"What do you want? Why are you calling me so early?" Kyle spoke into his phone.

"Good morning to you, too." Andrew laughed.

"Yeah, yeah."

"I called to remind you to make sure that you're at the airport on time tomorrow so we can make it to the meeting in L.A. with the Clippers front office."

"I didn't forget. I'll be on time."

"Why are you breathing so hard? I know you're not—"

"Naw, fool. I ain't having sex and talking to you." Kyle stopped running to laugh.

"Well, did you just finish?"

"No, fool. I'm out running." Kyle took deep breaths to slow down his heart rate.

"Oh, so you're out there chasing after that

sportscaster again." Andrew laughed.

"Yeah. I gotta go man."

"Okay. Just don't miss the plane tomorrow."

"Yeah, whatever." He sped off running again in hopes of catching Karen.

***

"Hey, Brian. Hey, Jeff. Hey, Nancy." Karen greeted her co-workers as she headed to her cubicle.

"Hey, Marge. Your husband must've either done something wrong or loves you a lot. There are so many flowers that you have them spread across my desk and yours." Karen rested her briefcase on her chair. She picked up a vase of flowers from her desk to squeeze onto Marge's desk, but Marge smirked and stopped her in her tracks.

"And why are you giving me that look?" Karen peeked from around the flowers.

The portly woman unfolded her arms from across her chest and braced her hands on her hips. "My husband didn't do anything wrong. These aren't from him or for me. They're for you. So how about you turn around and take them right back to your desk while I work to squeeze all of the ones on my desk onto yours." Marge turned on her heels and headed back to her desk laughing.

"For me?" Karen raised her eyebrows. "They can't possibly be for me."

"Well, they are. From some guy, initials K.I. I got tired after reading the first five cards attached to the flowers. They pretty much all say the same thing.

'Karen. Give me a chance. I like you...'"

"Wait, you read the cards and you knew they weren't for you?"

"Oh never mind that. You really did a number on this one. Has him paying you all of this attention. And I do mean 'paying', with how lovely and extravagant these arrangements are. I know he spent a pretty penny." Marge wobbled to her desk to answer the phone. "Hello, this is Marge speaking. How may I help you? Hold on." Marge put the call on mute. "Karen, there is a Kyle Irving wanting to speak with you."

Karen snapped her neck. Her eyes widened in disbelief as she walked towards Marge's desk. She mouthed to Marge, "Tell him I'm not here."

Marge furrowed her eyebrows. "Hello, I'm sorry, but she hasn't made it in for the day yet. Okay, I'll be sure to let her know you called. Okay. Have a great day."

Marge's smile widened as she looked up at Karen freaking out. "Calm down. Why are you so unnerved by this Kyle guy?"

"I'm not unnerved. I'm calm." Karen put her hands on her hips.

"Tell that to the sweat stains on your shirt."

Karen lowered her eyes in shame looking at the pit of her arms. "Okay. I met him running the other day. I admit that I was attracted to him until it hit me who he was."

"Well, who is he?"

"Marge, that was thee Kyle Irving of the Miami Heat."

Marge jumped to her feet as fast as she could given her girth. A fluorescent light bulb flickered above her head. "You mean that young, fine, Butterfinger glazed, muscular, tall drink of a man Kyle Irving of the Miami Heat? Speaking of Butterfingers, that reminds me to stop by the store on my way home to restock my snack drawer."

Karen laughed. "Yes, I mean no. I mean yes to the Kyle Irving part, not the fine, Butterfinger glazed, muscular, tall drink of a man part." Karen fanned herself.

Marge peeped over her glasses to look Karen in her eyes. "You're not fooling me. You've never fooled me. I can tell you like this man. That's why you're clearly doing so much to avoid him. Mmmh, can't tell me you're not." Marge continued to mumble under her breath as she headed back to her desk to resume her clerical duties.

"Well, I'm glad that I'll be leaving for my vacation in St. Lucia tomorrow so I can really 'avoid' him as you say." Karen's expression was pensive as she plopped in her seat. She picked a card from one of the bouquets. *Kyle Irving.* Her eyes smiled.

4

"Hurry up and finish getting dressed so that we can get good poolside seats for the midday pool bash," Karen said, gazing beyond the terrace of her hotel suite to the sea and pool.

"No rush. There will be plenty of men left to flirt with," Melanie said.

"You know I don't flirt with guys, and neither do you. We just talk a lot of smack about guys when they aren't around. How fine they are. How trifling some of them can be. You know, the usual."

"You're so silly." Melanie laughed. "Okay. I think I'm ready." She puckered her full lips in the mirror.

"I don't know why you take so much time getting ready when you barely wear any makeup. I mean really, twenty minutes for eyeliner, mascara, and clear lip gloss?" Karen rolled her almond shaped eyes at Melanie and opened the room door leading to the hallway.

They made silly faces in the mirrors of the elevator on the way down to the pool. They were still in silly mode making duck lips, sticking out their tongues, and crossing their eyes when the doors of the elevator opened and three handsome men spied them. They giggled profusely as they exited the elevator.

The men smirked as the doors closed.

***

So live your life
Hey, ayy, ayy, ayy
You steady chasin' that paper
Just live your life
Oh, ayy, ayy, ayy...

The voice of Rihanna, the pop singer, bellowed from the speakers as the ladies strolled down the stairs just outside of the hotel leading to the pool. They headed to the bar to the left of them seeing as though it was less crowded than the one on the other side.

"¡Oye! Mujeres bonitas. ¿Qué me das por ti?"

Karen and Melanie raised their eyebrows at one another.

"Que?" Karen's eyebrows lifted as if she had just gotten a Botox injection in them.

The bartender laughed. "You ladies no speak Spanish I see. What will you have?"

"Oh," Karen said and they laughed together.

"What do you suggest we have?" Melanie asked.

"For you bonitas, how about a Jaguar Colada?"

"Mmmh... What's in it?"

"Of course alcohol, but you can barely taste it. And then there's passion fruit, coconut crème."

Melanie hoped that she understood the ingredients of the drink through his thick accent. "Okay, one for her, and one for me. It better be good, Carlos." She stared at his nametag, and then winked at him.

He smiled at Melanie, and then started making their drinks while taking other customers orders.

Melanie smiled as she turned to look at her surroundings.

"Who are you eyeing like that?" Karen asked.

"No one in particular." Melanie winked at a dark beige man dancing across the pool.

He grabbed his drink and he and his friend and started walking her way.

She quickly turned around to face the bar and Karen. She tugged at Karen's wrist.

"What?"

"They're coming," Melanie whispered.

"Who's coming?"

"The man I winked at across the pool, and his friend."

"Are you scared or something?" Karen laughed. "Stop throwing bait if you don't want to catch something."

"Here you are mujeres bonitas!"

"Thank you," Karen spoke up and Melanie nodded her head in agreement.

"Excuse me. Hello." Mr. Dark-Beige tapped Melanie on her shoulder.

She slowly turned toward him with a mouthful of

her drink. She waved as she sipped more.

"Hi. My name is Malcolm, and this is my friend Raul." Malcolm swayed to the music while extending his hand to kiss Melanie's hand and then Karen's.

Raul simply nodded.

"Hi. My name is Karen, and this here little lamb is Melanie."

Melanie attentively nursed her drink.

Malcolm leaned in to whisper to Melanie. "Care to dance."

"I'm sorry, I can't leave my friend here alone."

"No worries, my drink will keep me company." Karen's smile widened to where almost all of her teeth were showing.

Melanie pinched Karen's wrist.

"So, will you dance with me?" Malcolm's eyes zoomed in on Melanie.

Melanie's nostrils flared as she stared at Karen. "You can dance with Raul."

Raul nodded and swayed to the music.

Karen looked at Malcolm. "What's up with him? He hasn't said a word."

Malcolm laughed. "He doesn't speak any English."

"Um, no thanks, Melanie. I'll tend to my drink while you dance with Malcolm."

Melanie snarled at Karen. "You know what, I'm not feeling so well." She placed her empty glass on the bar. "Sorry, Malcolm. I think I'm going to just go back to my room and lie down for a while." She grabbed Karen's wrist and pulled her away from the bar.

Malcolm and Raul stared at the ladies until they vanished from their vision.

Karen laughed and stopped Melanie in her tracks. "Where are we going? Because I am not going back up to the room with you, you party pooper."

"I'm not going upstairs either. I just said that to get away from them. Let's go on the other side of the hotel to the other pool party."

The ladies laughed as they shimmied down the beach attached to the resort in search of another party they were sure the hotel was hosting. Away from Raul and Malcolm.

***

Kyle, in his tailored Armani suit, stood gazing out of the window of the Staples Center office. There wasn't much scenery to look at other than Figueroa Street, the parking lot, or the lone glass skyscraper, but the view didn't matter to him anyway because his true vision was set on Karen back in Chicago.

"Kyle, come on. The meeting is about to start." Andrew tugged at Kyle's arm.

"Hello, gentlemen. So glad that you could come today," the Clippers general manager, Dave Wohl, said.

"Glad to be here," Andrew said and shook Clippers management hands as Kyle followed suit.

"We know that you have been receiving very attractive offers from other teams, but please bear in mind that we are the team that is almost guaranteed to come out of the West headed to the national finals. If we are already a contender with our current roster, we feel exceedingly confident that we will be the 2015 NBA Champions if we add you to our roster." Dave took his seat and smiled. "Oh, and let me add that you would be living here in beautiful California. We certainly can find you a home that fits your standards in Beverly Hills, Bel-Air, Brentwood, or any other neighborhood you would prefer."

Kyle sat there staring blankly at him.

Andrew spoke up, "Gentlemen, we know about the real-estate here, and we like who you already have on the roster. Our focus is your bottom line. How bad do you want Kyle Irving here?"

Kyle leaned back in his seat.

The general manager handed his scrawny, pale assistant a manila folder intended for Andrew and Kyle.

Andrew leaned in closer to Kyle as they reviewed the price the Clippers were willing to pay Kyle over the course of three years. Andrew's eyes widened in surprise.

Kyle remained demure.

The other gentlemen in the room sat back in their seats with confidence and smiles on their faces believing the money they offered and having a championship-contending team would make Kyle scream yes to their offer.

Kyle whispered into Andrew's ear.

Andrew lowered his head and shook it. His phone rang with an unfamiliar number but a Chicago area code. He showed Kyle the screen as if asking permission to take the call.

Kyle smiled and nodded at him.

"Excuse me, gentlemen. I have to take this call." Andrew stepped into the hallway.

"Get Mr. Irving something to drink." Dave motioned to his assistant.

"Here you are, Mr. Irving." He handed Kyle a bottle of Perrier water.

"Thank you. You can call me Kyle."

The young assistant's eyes sparkled. "Okay, Kyle."

Andrew reentered the board room. He sat down next to Kyle again and leaned in to whisper to him.

Kyle's face lit up with hope. Kyle whispered to him, and Andrew shook his head again in saddened shock.

Andrew closed the folder and turned toward the gentlemen. "Thank you all very much for your warm invitation to us today and this generous offer, but Kyle and I will need more time to discuss the logistics of this before we can give you our final response."

Dave was astonished. He stood and braced his hands on the table. He looked directly at Kyle. "Kyle, I can assure you that no other team in the West or even the league for that matter right now is capable of offering you what we are. Is there anything else we can or need to do to persuade you to be a Clipper this upcoming season?"

Kyle stood. "No, Mr. Wohl—"

"Please call me Dave." He overemphasized the warmth in his voice.

"Okay, Dave. Your offer and roster is very appealing. However, there are just some other things, people, that I have to take into consideration before I make my final decision." Kyle walked over and shook Dave's hand before he shook the other board members' hands. "Have a good day, gentlemen." He smiled and then walked out the door.

"I'm sorry, gentlemen, to have to cut this meeting so short, but you'll be hearing from us real soon." Andrew softly closed the door behind him.

They made it to the parking lot before Andrew felt free to talk. "What the hell, man? Even before I told you about the phone call, you should've been ready to pounce on their offer."

Kyle laughed. "Are you speaking as my agent or as my friend?" He removed his tie.

"Right now, a little bit of both."

"Okay friend-manager. Yes, they just offered me the most money that I would get from any team, and yes the Clippers are going to the finals next year, but so are the Bulls."

"But the money, man."

"You said it yourself that the Bulls have the next best offer money wise, so why not consider them?"

"Because you can get more money here in L.A., it's warmer, and because you can get more money."

"It's not all about the money. I can still win a ring in Chicago and…"

"And what?"

Kyle remained silent.

"Aww man." Andrew threw his hands up in the air and paced back and forth. "Don't tell me that you are letting this woman be your deciding factor for what team to join?"

"Don't worry about that. Let's just get back to Chicago for that meeting tonight."

They hopped in the car and rode off with the music blaring and Kyle singing Lalah Hathaway's slow jam, "I'm Coming Back", off key and as loud as he could.

5

"Please, will you turn that alarm off?" Melanie moaned as she rolled over pulling the covers over her head.

Karen laughed as she sat on the floor stretching her limbs.

"Turn it off."

"Nope."

"Ugh." Melanie rolled over in the bed to turn off the alarm on the night stand between her and Melanie's beds. "Why would you set an alarm when we're on vacation?" She nestled back under the covers.

"Just to annoy you." Karen laughed. "Besides it's nine a.m. We need to get down and enjoy our breakfast before they switch the menu to lunch."

"I don't care about breakfast. I just want at least another hour of sleep."

"What's wrong? A night filled with one too many Jaguar Colada's and hours of dancing with Malcolm has you tired?" Karen laughed.

Melanie threw a pillow at Karen's head, but she

missed her. "You promised never to bring him up again."

Karen laughed. "Sorry, I couldn't help myself. It's not my fault that he tracked you down on the other side of the hotel and you caved in, dancing and drinking with him the rest of the night."

"Oh shut up. Why don't you go run along the beach and leave me alone."

"Too late for that suggestion. I just came back from my run. It was great. You better be up by the time I get out of the shower or else…"

"Yeah, whatever. Just take your time."

The ladies laughed as Karen closed the bathroom door.

Melanie tried to grab a few more minutes of sleep.

***

"Did we really have to come here?" Andrew asked annoyed.

Kyle laughed. "You act like I brought you to Alaska or something. It's St. Lucia for heaven's sake. Just chill and enjoy yourself."

"How am I supposed to enjoy myself when you just cost me, us, some money last night? You just had to accept Chicago's offer even though it was nearly twenty million dollars less than what the Clippers offered you."

"I know." Kyle smirked.

"Man, I have kids to feed," Andrew said in a high-pitched voice.

Kyle almost spat out the liquor in his mouth. "Fool, stop lying. You ain't got no kids." He laughed and shook his head.

"Well, that money could've gone to my future kids. And why must you continue to chase this woman when clearly she doesn't want you? And how did you even know that she was here?"

"I called her office last night and luckily her assistant was still there. She kind of let it slip out that Karen was on vacation. So I worked my charm to find out where she was vacationing, which brings us here." Kyle smiled. "She doesn't know she wants me yet, but I plan to change that."

"Aw, okay playa. You 'charmed' the assistant, and now you're plotting on what's her name, Karen? I thought you said those days were over?"

"They are. I simply told the assistant that I would bring over a signed basketball for her son. And I'm not chasing Karen just to hit it and quit it. I really want to get to know her. I think she could be the one."

"Oh, 'the one'. So you think that there is only one woman out there for you, man?"

"Naw, I wouldn't say that. I just think that she's the one for me. She makes sense to me."

"But you don't even know her."

"I know what I feel and that's why I'm here."

"Man, don't confuse gas with love. You're just lusting after her." Andrew shook his head. "Look." He pointed across the pool. "She ain't checking for you. She's too busy checking for him."

***

Karen laughed hysterically and leaned into Dennis. His firm muscles and warm skin alerted her womanly senses. She eased back from him and ran her fingers through her hair to recompose herself. She never looked at him this way before. *Maybe it's the sun hitting my skin? The sound of the waves rushing on the sands? Or is it just that I haven't been this close to a man like him in such a long time? Oh well, I'll try to enjoy this moment while I can.*

The laugh lines around Dennis's eyes creased more and more as he stared at Karen.

Melanie noticed the exchange.

"Dennis, you are soooo silly," Karen blurted out in response to the corny joke that Dennis had told.

Melanie feigned laughing.

"It's such a coincidence running into you here." Dennis stared intently at Karen.

She blushed. "Coincidence? I don't think so. Don't you remember me telling you a couple of weeks back that I would be vacationing here this week?"

Melanie pursed her lips and squinted her eyes.

"Oh, did you? I must've forgotten. My boys and I just picked a place on the globe and caught a flight out." He coughed and cleared his throat.

"I bet," Melanie said under her breath.

Karen pinched her arm.

Melanie pinched her back.

"You two okay?" Dennis stared between the two

of them.

"Yeah, I was just trying to get a bug off of her." Melanie said trying to hide her merriment.

"So would you two like to—" Dennis was interrupted.

"Hi, Karen. Hi, Melanie." The bass in Kyle's voice sent tremors down Karen's spine. Her pupils dilated. Her heart beat hastened. *Damn! Marge was right. Why does his presence unnerve me?* She pushed her hair out of her face and stood up straighter.

Melanie gulped down the laughter in her throat.

"Kyle." Karen snarled at him. "What are you doing here? Are you following me again?"

Kyle smiled. He knew her words didn't match her body's response to him.

"Following you? No. I'm on vacation."

"Yeah, we're on vacation." Andrew formed his words slowly as he stared at Melanie. *Her eyes.*

Melanie was too focused on the interaction between Karen and Kyle to notice Andrew's interest in her.

"Oh, my bad. Karen, Melanie, you." Kyle glanced at Dennis. "This is my friend slash agent, Andrew. Andrew, this is Karen, Melanie, and—"

"I'm Dennis." He shook Kyle's hand. They battled who could hold the firmest grip, at least until Karen pulled their hands apart.

"Say bruh, would you mind moving over to the other side of the pool? The sun's glare on your head is kind of blinding." Dennis laughed heartily at his joke.

Kyle squared his shoulders.

Melanie finally shifted her attention to Andrew. She liked what she saw.

Dennis continued to laugh and sipped some of his drink.

"Kyle, Dennis is a fellow sportscaster with my network, but I'm pretty sure you know that." Karen squinted her eyes at Kyle.

"Uh, no. I actually didn't recognize him without all the makeup."

"Wa—"

"Gentlemen." Karen raised one eyebrow as she pleaded firmly with them.

Kyle and Dennis backed down from one another.

"So many coincidences today. Anywho, how are you doing, Kyle?" Melanie smiled as she spoke.

Andrew's stare deepened into Melanie.

"I'm good. Really just came down here to enjoy the view." Kyle looked at Karen and took a long sip of his drink.

"Melanie, remember we have our spa appointments in ten minutes? We better hurry, we don't want to be late," Karen said.

"Hunh?" Melanie struggled to pull her attention away from Andrew.

"You remember, don't you, Melanie?" Karen pressed her lips together.

Melanie paused, her eyes searching for understanding in Karen's. "Oh, yeah, we do have a spa appointment, but remember, it's not until tomorrow." Melanie laughed.

Karen's nostrils flared. Her stare bore holes

through Melanie.

"Melanie, you want to go get another drink?" Andrew extended his hand out to her.

"Sure." She smiled. "I'll be back, Karen."

As she walked away, Karen yelled, "Melanie. Melanie. Melanie."

Melanie laughed, ignoring Karen.

"So, Karen." both Kyle and Dennis said in unison.

"Yes, Dennis?"

Kyle stood quietly glaring at her, unwavered.

"Let's say you and I head to the bar where we can continue our conversation, alone?" Dennis asked.

"Sure—"

"Hey, man, come run point for me." Dennis's friend ran up to the threesome.

Dennis turned to him and mumbled under his breath, "Man, not now."

"Come on, man." The desperation in his friend's voice rang out loud.

"Shoot, okay." Dennis turned towards Karen. "I'll be right back. Don't go anywhere." He squeezed her hand.

"No rush. Take your time." Kyle smirked.

Dennis headed towards Kyle, but his friend tugging on his arm caused him to retreat.

"I'll be back, Karen," Dennis said over his shoulder.

"Now that he's gone, let's say you and I take a stroll along the beach." Kyle extended his arm out signaling that she should walk ahead of him through the crowd.

Karen hesitated.

"Please?" Kyle pouted. "I don't bite."

"I'm not scared, but if you did bite, my Taser would calm you down." Karen walked ahead of him.

Kyle shook his head and smiled.

***

We found love in a hopeless place
We found love in a hopeless place
We found love in a hopeless place
We found love in a hopeless place

The DJ was playing another Rihanna party song. Bikini-clad women jumped up and down all around the pool while the men nodded their heads to the music and nodded in approval of the women bouncing up and down around them.

Melanie slowly sipped her drink and bobbed her head as she stared into the crowd.

Andrew's stare penetrated her senses.

"What?" she said to Andrew.

His eyebrows lifted. He shook his head as he said, "You are just beautiful. It's something about your eyes. They seem so familiar, and yet I can't recall from where."

"Thanks. And are you saying that my eyes remind you of an ex-girlfriend?" She said.

"No. From someone in my past. I just don't know who."

"Speaking of pasts, tell me about yours." Melanie angled her body completely towards his. She put on her sunglasses to dim the sun's intensity.

"Please don't…"

"What?"

"I want to look into your eyes."

Melanie's chocolaty complexion couldn't hide her blushing cheeks.

"I'll switch seats with you." Andrew got up from his chair and helped Melanie from hers before they switched seats. "Better?"

"Yes. Thank you. So are you ready to tell me about your past now? More about yourself?"

"What do you want to know?"

"Whatever you're comfortable telling me about. Ex-wives, how many kids you have, arrest record? You know, the usual." Melanie raised one eyebrow.

"That's the usual for you?" His forehead creased as he frowned.

Melanie laughed. "Not for me. But that's the norm nowadays for men."

Andrew shook his head as he smiled at Melanie. "Well, my full name is Andrew Dodson, no middle name. Never been arrested. No ex-wives. No kids. Every graduation I had, I was at the top of my class. I love being a sports agent. I don't ever want to retire from it. I want to do it 'til the day I die. I get such a thrill from closing deals for my clients."

"Okay." Melanie smiled at his clean record. "So tell me about your family."

"Let's see, I was adopted, and I have an older brother and a younger sister from my adopted family. I don't know anything about my birth family." Andrew cast his eyes down.

Melanie patted him on his knee. "I'm sorry about that. Seems like you wish you did."

"Yeah, my mom gave me up for adoption when I was like four. I don't know why. I can only remember her being sad and depressed all the time."

"You seem to have turned out great, so your adoptive family must be amazing."

"Yeah they really are. I just have always had this longing to know my birth family, especially my mom. I often wonder if she's okay. Did she have any more kids?"

"So why haven't you tried to find out more about your birth family?"

"Trust me, I tried, but since it was a closed adoption, they seriously refuse to give me any information about my birth mother or father."

"I'm sorry that I asked about your family since it seems to make you sad."

"No, that's okay. It's a part of getting to know me, but I know what could make me smile."

"What?" Melanie eyed him suspiciously.

"Let's flip the script, and you tell me more about you." Andrew perked up.

"Well, my name is Melanie Daniels. I am a connoisseur of good art. I'm an artist and I own my own art gallery. I've never been married before. Never really had a serious relationship. No kids. I honestly do love running, I just like to make Karen think that I don't." Melanie laughed.

"Wait, did you say that you've never been in a relationship?" Andrew's eyes widened.

"Uh, yeah."

"That's shocking. A woman like yourself, I would think that you're barely ever single." He cleared his throat. "My bad, I didn't even ask if you're dating someone now. Are you?"

"No, I'm not."

"So why are you single?"

Melanie hesitated before speaking. "My mom."

"What about her?"

"Just some things that she's told me about men and relationships over the years about being extra careful with them and how attentive I have to be with her leaves me little time for a relationship."

"What things?"

"I don't want to talk about it now." Melanie's eyes shifted back and forth. "Let's go find Kyle and Karen."

***

"Now that's funny." Karen held her stomach as she walked. Her abdomen muscles seemed to hurt from laughing so much with Kyle.

"It wasn't funny then, but I'm glad you're getting a kick out of my rookie mistakes. You really do have a beautiful smile." Kyle stared at her.

She turned and stared at the clear, glistening water trying to hide her smile.

"Karen?"

"What?" She didn't turn back towards him.

"Karen, I'm not as bad as you thought I was, am I?"

Karen spoke in a flat voice. "No, I guess not." But

a smile soon crept on her face.

"So you'll give me a chance?" Kyle tugged at her arm until she faced him again.

"I didn't say all of that."

"Seriously, will you?"

"Only time will tell."

They continued walking along the beach until they reached an eroded rock, which seemed to be a nature made bench.

"Let's sit here," Kyle suggested.

"Okay." Karen brushed her hair out of her face.

Karen normally drilled men who wanted her attention, but the landscaping of the sand and the blue hues of the sea along with Kyle's magnetic presence suspended her desire to drill him. She sat silent for a moment enjoying nature and his presence.

Kyle stared at her looking off into the sea. "What are you thinking about?"

"Mmh?" Karen looked at him and her heart beat faster. Kyle was staring at her with the same admiration in his eyes that she always saw her father gaze at her mother. Kyle's stare pulled on her heart.

"You okay?" He scooted closer to her and rubbed her arm, hoping to soothe the goose bumps that formed on them.

"Yeah, I'm okay." She allowed herself to stare into his eyes for some time before she turned away.

"Karen, you can talk to me about whatever it is that has you unsettled right now. Let me know if I did or said something wrong so that I can make it right."

Karen gave him a half smile. "No, you didn't say anything wrong."

"Well, what did I do then?" Kyle turned his body more towards hers.

"It's nothing really. You just looked at me the way my dad used to look at my mom." A tear escaped her eye.

"Used to? What happened? They got a divorce?"

"No. They died."

Kyle didn't know what to say. He couldn't imagine living without his parents. "I'm sorry, Karen."

"Don't be." She smiled. "You didn't cause their death."

"So what did?"

Karen remained silent.

"If you don't want to talk about it, you don't have to."

Karen had never given any other man the full story of her life.

Kyle interlocked his hand with hers as they silently watched the waves dance.

She hated to admit it so soon to herself, but she was so comfortable with him. She was ready to share her story with him. "I was sixteen, a junior in high school and on the basketball team. We were in the championship game downstate. Of course, I rode the bus with my team, and my parents drove to the game as they always did." She wiped tears from her eyes. "Long story short, I had just come down from the ladder cutting the net because we had won and we were taking it back with us. My coach pulled me off to the side to tell me that my parents never made it to the game because they had died in a car crash on the way."

Kyle pulled her closer to him trying to calm her trembling body.

"I don't know why I still cry whenever I think about that day. I mean, look at me. I'm doing great for myself, aren't I?"

Kyle let her rhetorical question linger in the air.

"I was an only child, and so were my parents. The only living relative I had was my older cousin, Janice, who took me in and raised me during my last year of high school, but she died while I was in college. Melanie, her mom, and her dad are like my only family."

"Thanks for sharing that with me."

"I didn't plan to, but when I looked into your eyes I saw my dad looking at my mom. I felt at peace with sharing it with you."

"You smile whenever you mention the way he looked at her. Tell me more about them, their love."

Karen smiled and rid her face of any trace of tears. "My father was a hardworking man, but he always made time for me and my mom. I acted like I was grossed out with how affectionate they were to each other, but it really did show me how a man should look at a woman, how he should treat her. That's why I won't let you or any other man do me any kind of way."

"What other men?" Kyle's face scrunched up.

"Don't worry about that." Karen jumped up from the rock and walked closer to the water. "I know what love looks like. I saw it for sixteen years."

"Whoa. Hold on. I'm not looking to hurt you, Karen." Kyle walked in front of her. "I like you a lot, and my interest in you is growing by the second."

"Mmmm hmmm." Karen twisted her lips.

Kyle smiled. "Whatever."

"Don't look at me that way."

"What way? The same way your dad looked at your mom?" Kyle's stare intensified. "You know they say the eyes are the windows to a person's soul."

He pulled Karen closer to him and just stared in her eyes.

Her body relaxed in his arms.

***

Dennis kneeled behind a big rock further down the shore. *That should be me holding Karen like it should've been me consoling her at her parent's funeral instead of the star basketball player at our high school. I won't be the last man standing this time. Gloves off! No more Mr. Nice Guy.*

6

"I see you've come to terms with how much you like Kyle." Melanie teased Karen as she lowered the lid on the toilet and sat on it.

Karen pretended as if she hadn't heard Melanie as her short framed leaned further over the counter to be closer to the mirror. She tilted her head back slightly as she applied her extra black mascara giving special attention to almost every single hair of her eyelashes.

"Ignore me all you want, but you know I'm telling the truth. I mean really, your eyelashes are already long, but with the attention you're giving them with that mascara, you're definitely going for a dramatic look. And you'd only do that if you wanted to be appealing to a certain someone." Melanie crossed one long, slender leg over the other and leaned back against the pinstriped wallpapered wall to get a better look at Karen.

Satisfied with the pop affect her luscious lashes gave her eyes, Karen resealed her mascara tube and grabbed her lip gloss.

"Karen, stop ignoring me."

Karen puckered one last time and evened out the gloss on her lips before she turned to face Melanie. She braced her hip on the counter top and her hands on her hip. "It only makes sense to ignore you, because when I tell you that I'm not into him as you say I am, you keep going on and on and on that I am. So why should I interrupt your crazy fest? I'll let you hash that out on your own." Karen smirked and pivoted on her sandal clad heels before she exited the bathroom.

Melanie was instantly behind her. "Whatever. You'll tell me soon enough just how attracted to him you are, even though I already know it. I don't know why you act like I don't know when you're lying or holding something back. We've known each other too long not to know otherwise." Melanie flopped down on the bed and pulled a pillow onto her chest.

Karen shook her head as she put her diamond studs in her ears.

"So where are you all going anyway?"

"I don't know. He just asked me to be ready at eight."

Melanie rolled over on her stomach and stared at Karen with dreamy eyes. "A secretive date. Oh, this should be good "

"No one said this was a date." Karen averted eye contact with Melanie.

"No, it's not a date, and my name is not Melanie Daniels, it's Betty White."

Karen whipped her neck at Melanie and stared at her incredulously before they both buckled over with laughter.

"Really? Don't bring one of the Golden Girls into this."

"Well, the girl in this room with me needs to stop lying to herself because she ain't getting nothing over on me. I don't know why you feel like you have to be in control all of the time." Melanie instantly tightened her mouth wishing she could take back what she said. She knew exactly why Karen felt she needed to be in control all of the time. "Karen, I—"

Karen dismissively waved at Melanie as she put her lip gloss in her clutch bag. "Don't worry about it. As you said, you know me and I know me, too, so we'll leave my 'control' issues out of this conversation." Karen tightened the spaghetti straps on her coral sundress.

Melanie was glad they wouldn't have to rehash Karen's past. She took delight in refocusing the conversation as she sat up in her bed. "So, you don't know where you two are going and you think that a dress is your best choice of clothing? What if he wants to do something adventurous tonight?"

"Not sure exactly what he has planned for tonight as he said it was a surprise, but we're going ziplining tomorrow, hiking the day after, snorkeling, and then volcano exploring. Tonight is the only night I don't have the specifics for." Karen found herself smiling with anticipation, but she soon wiped the smile from her face. She didn't need her emotions getting ahead of her. She needed to be level headed with a guy like Kyle.

Melanie's eyes widened. "I'm impressed that he's

mapped out the rest of the week with you, but from the sound of it, you and I won't get a chance to hang out together, since this was after all our girls' getaway." Melanie feigned sadness with the pout of her lips.

"Don't act as if you won't be preoccupied with Andrew," Karen said.

Melanie's lips curved into a wry smile.

"Exactly, so while I'm just 'hanging' out with Kyle, you'll continue to be engrossed in Andrew as you have been," Karen said matter-of-factly.

"He is fine, isn't he?" Melanie smirked.

"I wouldn't know, I ain't checkin' for him."

There was a knock at the door.

"As you shouldn't be. Besides, you can't see past Kyle anyway," Melanie said as she rushed from her bed to answer the door before Karen could.

"I don't know why we didn't get separate rooms," Karen said as she gave up the battle to beat Melanie to the door.

"Because you knew it'd be more fun this way, but I'm guessing your real fun is at the door."

***

Kyle stepped aside and let Karen enter the elevator before he did.

"Thank you." She nodded her head and then stepped in.

He rushed in and collided with her pinning her against the wall.

Her breathing was shallow as she stared up into

his eyes. His closeness was too much for her senses. "Kyle?"

"What?" He chuckled as he braced one arm on the wall behind her and the other still remaining on her hip.

"You know what. This." She wedged her hand in between and motioned it back and forth.

"The door was going to close on me. I fell into you when I jumped in. You didn't want me to get smashed by the door or something, did you?"

One eyebrow inquisitively raised at him.

He stared right back into those dark brown eyes of hers hoping her interest in him mirrored his attraction to her.

Her breathing became even more shallow, and she pushed him back from her.

Kyle held her flattened palm to his chest as she kept her arm extended between them. He smiled inwardly watching how his stare was unnerving her. He was glad to see some kind of sign that she liked him. It only made him more excited for the plans he made for them for the rest of the week. He needed every moment he spent with her to show her just how attracted he was to her.

He kissed her palm, to which she squirmed. He smiled at her as the elevator door opened and he pulled her out with him. "This way." He fell in stride next to her and interlocked his hand with hers as they walked through an exit and down a lit path towards the beach. His smile settled as he realized she hadn't pulled her hand out of his.

The sun had set hours before and the sky was

pitch dark. The waves slowly caressing the shore provided a mellow soundtrack to their stroll along the beach before Kyle broke the comfortable silence between them. "You okay?"

"I'm great." Karen was barely audible as she worked to hide the glee in her voice. She didn't even know what he had in store for them, but in addition to the time they'd already spent together at the resort and capped off by the peaceful stroll with him along the beach, he was making it hard for her not to like him.

So far he wasn't panning out the way she thought he would—a dog. But that still didn't mean that she had to let her guard down with him, just yet. If ever. Her breath caught in her throat as he tickled the palm of her hand by gliding his middle finger across it.

Judging by how she looked off at the water, he didn't know just what type of effect the mindless gesture was having on her.

The tickling of her palm, which had become so comforting to her, and his manly scent that she inhaled every time a wave hit the shore drew her closer to him. She gripped his arm and drifted closer to him, leaning her head on his shoulder before flickering lights on the water caught her attention. "What's that?" She pointed towards the water.

"My surprise for you." Kyle squeezed her hand as they approached a pier. He led her to the gazebo perched at the end of it.

She stopped short of the structure framing the beautiful scene. She pulled her hand from his and cupped her face as she stopped in her tracks. "Kyle."

Her voice was airy.

"What?" His eyebrows furrowed as worry lines marred her beautiful face.

"This is…too much." She shook her head looking up at him.

"I don't think so." He gazed at her.

"But—"

"But let's just enjoy the night. Please?" He held out his hand to her.

She couldn't reject the tender plea in his voice even if she tried to. "Okay." She placed her hand in his as he guided her up the half step.

He led her to the table and pulled back the chair, helping her to be seated. He soon sat across from her.

"Kyle, how'd you get all of this together so soon?" She turned from his attentive gaze to stare at what seemed like a hundred white votive candles framing the floor and railings of the gazebo. Their vanilla scent mixed in with the sea breeze calmed her as she stared at the flickering lights. The moonlight reflecting off the water only further serenaded her. It all was a sight she hadn't seen in a long time. A feeling she hadn't felt in a long time.

She looked so peaceful andKyle was in no rush to stop her from taking in the moment.

She finally pulled her eyes from the scene around her and tuned back to Kyle. She braced her elbows on the table and rested her chin on her interlaced hands. "How and why?"

"How? I had the front desk to help me set this up." Kyle turned his head and nodded to a waiter who held platters of food.

Karen simply smiled as she sat back and allowed the man to fill their table with food.

"Will that be all, sir?"

"Yes." Kyle nodded to the man. "And that's for the wine, too." Kyle pointed to the bottle of wine chilling in a wine bucket on a stand. He knew it took the man some doing to get him the specific brand of wine he asked for.

"No problem, sir."

Kyle shook the man's hand and placed a handsome tip in it.

He looked at the money and nodded vigorously at Kyle as he backed away from the table and walked away.

Karen simply stared at him. He didn't mind it either. Ever since he'd met her, she'd been doing a great job not paying him much mind, so to have her attention thrilled him. Besides, he loved looking into her eyes.

When Karen could no longer take the intense stare between her and Kyle she spoke up again. "Okay, so I know you have the means for the how, but why?"

"Why? Karen, for you, why not? Why wouldn't I wanna do something special for you? I know we're just getting to know each other, but from what I've gathered about you, you don't take much time to just enjoy yourself."

She sat back with a look of indifference and pondered his assessment.

"You're so career-driven and goal-oriented that

you probably don't pamper yourself the way you should."

Karen cocked her head at him. "So you think you know me?"

"Not as much as I would like to get to know you. I wanna spoil you, Karen." He reached over and caressed her hand that rested on the table.

Karen stared into his eyes, replaying what he'd just said and saw pure honesty shone in them. Again, he was dulling her senses and she needed to regain her composure. She pulled her hand away from his embrace. "Kyle, I don't need you to take care of me. I can take care of myself. Besides, with the life you live, you don't have much time for me." She sat back and folded her arms across her chest. She knew she needed to keep the wall she had built around herself erect.

"Karen," Kyle leaned forward, "I know you can take care of yourself. That's why I'm not saying spoil you with things, but with my time, attention, and affection. Yeah, I'm as busy with my career as you are with yours, but because I want you, I'll make time for you."

The depth of which he said "make" pricked holes in the bubble Karen had placed herself in. His intentional voice, his unwavering eyes, and his relaxed yet stern body language attested to the sincerity of his words.

She just couldn't be possessed by this man so suddenly. She leaned forward and stared directly at him. "What are we having for dinner?"

Kyle laughed as he pulled the stainless-steel lids

from the plates on the table. "That's okay, I'll just keep showing you how serious I am about you."

"Please don't," Karen mumbled to herself as he uncovered what they'd be eating.

Their eyes danced with one another the rest of the dinner as they sipped wine. Karen worked to avoid certain topics and questions from Kyle for about an hour. They had the opportunity to learn much more about each other's childhoods via the stories they shared with one another.

"That was good." Kyle rubbed his stomach and leaned back in his chair.

"Yes, it was. Thank you." Karen genuinely smiled at him.

"My pleasure. Did you enjoy yourself?" Kyle asked as he stood and stretched.

Karen followed suit. "I did."

"You ready to go, or do you mind staying out here with me longer?" Kyle inched closer to Karen.

The table had provided much needed distance between them, but now that Kyle stood in front of her, there was nothing to impede the chemistry between them. "Kyle?"

"What, Karen?" He inched closer to her and began caressing her arms as he stared into her eyes.

"Kyle..." Lost in his eyes, that was all she could manage to say.

"You cold?" He felt the goosebumps on her arm. He had a suspicion of their cause, but he asked anyway, seeing if she would be honest with him. Her standoffish demeanor with him most of the time was both exciting and frustrating. On one hand, he enjoyed Karen not being so emotionally accessible to him like the women that threw themselves at him, but on the other hand, he wished she could see just how sincere his interest in her was and let her guard down.

"Yeah." She lied.

"You sure." His deep voice was husky as he lowered his head, causing his lips to hover inches above hers.

Her chest heaved up and down. She bit her lip, anticipating him kissing her, but reasoning kicked in and redirected her thoughts, her needs. "Just walk me back to my room please." She quickly turned away from him and headed back down the pier.

7

"Why are we out here so early in the morning?" Melanie's head dropped to the side as she laid on her sling chaise lounge and stared at Karen. The sun was blaring down on them but it only hit from their knees and below since they had umbrellas pitched in the sand hovering over them.

People were already out in the sea swimming and frolicking in the salty water. Runners kicked up sand as they sprinted along the beach.

"You agreed to eat breakfast with me before I head out with Kyle."

"Oh yeah, I did." Melanie shrugged her shoulders and then chuckled at herself.

"Silly. You complained about possibly not seeing me that much the rest of the trip with all of the things Kyle has planned for us." Karen sighed and her shoulders sloped.

Melanie turned on her side. "Why do you sound so darg near depressed saying that? Do you know how many women would kill to have Kyle Irving swooning after them the way he is after you?"

Melanie turned on her side and rested her head in her hand to get a better read on Karen.

Karen laid back with her sunglasses on and mindlessly crossed one ankle on top of the other, repeatedly. "I don't care about them. It's too much, too soon from him. Just like you said, with all the women that would kill to be with Kyle Irving, I can't expect him to be faithful to me." Karen folded her arms tightly across her chest.

"So, did last night give you a better indication of what kind of man he is?"

Karen bit her lip remembering the way he tickled her palm with his finger. It was so endearing to her, but she knew every man knew how to worm his way into a woman's life if he wanted to. She wouldn't let her guard down with him. Especially not the likes of Kyle Irving. Been there, done that. She wouldn't play herself again with a professional athlete.

"Karen?"

"What?"

"Did he? Did you get a better sense last night of the kind of man he is?"

"Yes, but—"

"But nothing. Just give the man a chance."

"Exactly. Just give me a chance," Dennis said as he walked up and interrupted their conversation. "You should listen to your best friend." He stared at Karen.

A corner of Melanie's mouth curved up as she stared at him. Annoyed by his presence. Annoyed that he inserted himself in their conversation. Annoyed that he was blocking her gorgeous view of the clear waters and the brilliant blue sky. She was annoyed by everything about him, especially how he just kept popping up on them. "I wasn't talking about you," she mumbled and turned her head. She didn't want to look at him any longer.

With Karen's legs drawn into her chest, Dennis made himself comfortable sitting at the end of her sling chaise lounge.

"So, I didn't see you again yesterday. I was looking for you."

"I was busy," Karen said, pulling her T-shirt out her bag and putting it on top of her bikini top. She sat upright, adjusting it.

"How about you and I hang out today? Take in some sights on the island?" His voice oozed with hope.

Melanie rolled over anxious to speak up before Karen could respond. "She can't. She has plans already."

"Well maybe my friend can tag along with us and keep you company then, Melanie?" Dennis faced Melanie.

"Oh, she doesn't have plans with me. She'll be tied up with Kyle all day, the rest of the week. Not the S and M kind of tied up. At least I don't think so." Melanie stared at Karen pretending to question how exactly she'd be tied up with Kyle.

Karen's eyes narrowed in on Melanie and she pressed her lips tightly together not being able to say exactly what she wanted to Melanie in front of Dennis.

Melanie gave Karen a wide, closed mouth smile as she stared back at Karen. She wiggled her eyebrows at her for good measure.

After hearing Melanie's response, Dennis worked diligently to keep the scowl from appearing on his face. He was tired of this Kyle character interrupting his chances to spend time with Karen. But he wouldn't give up. "So, there's no chance of me spending some time with you today?"

"Nope," Kyle said in a deep, definitive voice as he walked up and stood near Karen. He didn't even bother to look at Dennis. "You ready to head out, Karen?"

She looked up at him admiring the way his tank top lay on his sculpted torso. His muscles flexed as he stretched his arm out to help her up. "Sure." Her throat was dry and she wasn't even sure the word came out as she placed her hand in his and stood.

She was barely able to get her footing before Kyle pulled her into his arms for a hug. He nestled his face in the crook of her neck and audibly inhaled her scent. "You smell so good," he whispered in her ear, refusing to release her from his arms.

The gesture stunned Karen but sent shivers down her spine and heat pooled between her legs. *How can I resist him when he hugs me like this?* Karen yielded to her desires for the moment and wrapped her arms around his neck, which made him squeeze her even tighter.

With her head against his chest, she had a front row seat to the inebriating scent that had her restless the night before.

Kyle hesitantly lowered her to her feet as he intently stared into her eyes. He wanted to show her every chance he looked into them just how into her he was. She held his gaze for a moment. Her small, pouty lips parted as if she wanted to say something, but she quickly looked away from him and stepped out of his embrace.

She took a deep breath to calm her senses before she reached down to grab her bag. When she lifted back up she saw the mocking glee on Melanie's face. She shook her head at Melanie and pointed a strong finger at her.

Melanie's head titled to the side and she shrugged her shoulders as she forced her hands high as if to say. "What did I do?"

As much as Dennis wanted to pounce on Kyle for interrupting his conversation with Karen and embracing her the way he did, he figured Karen wouldn't take a liking to the action, so he quietly bid his time.

Kyle lifted a daring eyebrow at Dennis as he sensed his disdain for him.

Karen was staring at Melanie and unaware of the staring match between Kyle and Dennis as Dennis stood to his feet working to subdue his anger of Kyle's challenging stare.

"You ready?" Kyle asked Karen as he steadied one arm around her waist.

"Yeah. Bye, Mel. Bye, Dennis." She looked back at both of them as she settled her purse on her shoulder and walked ahead of Kyle with his hands planted on her waist.

Kyle looked back over his shoulder and said, "Bye, Melanie."

She laughed and waved at them. "Bye, Karen. Bye, Kyle."

Still looking over his shoulder, Kyle glared at Dennis with a menacing smirk and said, "Bye, Darren."

Dennis clenched his fists and gritted his teeth. "It's Dennis. My name is Dennis."

***

Karen sat as still as she could on the bus and stared out the window. They were headed to where they'd be ziplining. Kyle sat next to her with his arm stretched out behind her, and every so often he'd squeeze or rub her shoulder. After she looked at him the first two times he did it, she realized the gesture seemed second nature to her rather than trying to get her attention.

She kept her knees together to prevent her leg from touching his. Every time it hit his, her body reacted, and not in a way she wanted it to. She was willing to explore the island with him, but not like him. Touching him, being so close to him was making that hard for her.

She sank into her seat and stared out the window enjoying the beautiful scenery when her leg fell against his again. He squeezed it and kissed her forehead. She froze as he let his lips and the stubble from his chin linger against her smooth skin before he pulled back some from her.

Unsure of what to say or do, she slowly looked up to his eyes. They were innocent and unassuming. He smiled at her and then fixed his gaze back on the mix of colors of the flowers and trees native to the island. The beautiful array was dispersed among the colorful and varying shaped houses they saw en route to the site where they would zipline.

His calm soothed and alarmed her at the same time. She looked at him again staring out the window. "Kyle?" Her voice was low and throaty.

"Hunh?" Coming out of his reverie, he stared into her eyes.

"Why'd you just kiss my forehead?" She shook her head, admitting that the question sounded juvenile, but she needed to make sense of his actions. Plus, she was never one to beat around the bush.

"Because it just felt right. Being here with you just feels right." He squeezed her shoulders again.

"You're different?"

Kyle lifted one eyebrow as a subtle laugh escaped him. "What do you mean?"

"I mean, talking with you the other day on the beach, the candlelit dinner with you last night, and this now." She pointed between the two of them. "You're so serene, chill, not like the way you are on the court or portrayed in the media."

"Karen, you're not my opponent."

She bit her bottom lip and stared into his eyes as he spoke. His words sounded so sincere. His voice so soothing. His closeness so enchanting.

"I have no need to be aggressive with you. And as far as how I'm portrayed in the media, I left my bad boy ways alone, a long time ago. I told you, don't lump me with all the other athletes."

She turned her head away from him, from his words, and moved closer to the window.

He chuckled as he closed in on her and rested his chin on her shoulder blade. "You can keep running if you want to, I'll only keep chasing you."

She was scared to look at him. She could feel the sensual heat of his breath on her face and knew that if she turned to him, a kiss was inevitable.

If she were to be honest with herself, which she had no intention of doing in his case, she would admit that since they'd been on the island, she toyed with the idea of kissing him. But every time the reality of who he was confronted her, she pushed aside any interest she might have in him.

"We're here ladies and gentleman," the shuttle driver announced as he parked the bus.

Kyle's sensual breaths had been tickling the sensitive spot behind her ear for quite some time. She was tingling all over. She took a deep breath trying to calm her senses. "Kyle, it's time for us to get off," she whispered as she kept her face angled towards the window. Kyle hadn't budged from his chest pressing into her back.

"Okay." He smiled against her cheek. Her posture was rigid and he reasoned she was trying to stay in control of herself around him. "So face me." His head fell back in laughter.

Karen used the opportunity to turn and playfully shove him away from her as she stood. Her plan didn't work. Kyle grabbed her wrists and pulled her into him.

She was wedged between the seat behind her and Kyle's firm body in front of her. The body she practically laid on as she stared into the deep dark brown pools of his eyes. *How much more can I take of this?*

Kyle stared at her lips as she stared at his. His breathing became audible and he leaned in to her, but flashbacks of the men from her past glossed before her eyes and she sprang up from Kyle. "Only ziplining for us today, Mr. Irving." Sass dripped from her voice as she scurried from their row and off the bus.

Kyle shook his head, staring at her as she walked away. "She's worth the chase," he mumbled to himself as he left the bus.

8

Karen couldn't contain her smile as she stepped into the elevator back at the hotel. Aside from being covered in dirt and her heart beating erratically every time Kyle got close to her as if he was trying kiss her, she really enjoyed ziplining and dining with him. Kyle was genuinely funny and seemed to do whatever he could to keep her laughing.

But it was those intense stare-offs she found herself in with him that reminded her to keep any real interest in him subdued.

The deliberate way he stared at her each time was enough to accept any offer he shot her way. Like the look he was giving her as he leaned on the back wall of the elevator.

"What?" Humor tinted her voice as she looked up at him.

"Nothing. I just like staring at you."

"Suit yourself then." Karen faced the elevator doors. She held a straight face as long as she could before the laughter gracing her eyes spewed out of her.

"I love that about you." He stood up straight and shoved his hands in his pockets.

"What?" She found herself patting her hair.

"That ability of yours to switch from being sarcastic to silly so quickly. I know you're not as tough as you make yourself out to be."

"Whatever."

The elevator doors opened. They stepped out and fell into stride next to one another as they silently walked to Karen's door.

They made it there and Karen began shuffling through her purse looking for her room key.

"So, I guess this is goodnight, hunh?" Kyle found himself stuttering like a young schoolboy waiting for his crush to respond to a note he sent her in class.

"Yeah, I guess so." Karen located her room key. Avoiding eye contact with Kyle, she stared at the key as if she were staring at a prized diamond.

"Well, sweet dreams," he said, but his feet didn't move.

"Not just yet. Today was tiring and I think the best way to end it would be if I shower really quickly and then sit in the hot tub downstairs for a while." Karen tapped her card on the keycard lock and twisted the knob.

"How about I join you?"

Karen didn't push the door in though. She was stumped by Kyle's question.

She was eager to get in the hot tub, hoping the jets would massage all the anxiety she harbored from blocking all the advances he made. But on the other hand, she wasn't ready to end her night with him just yet. She cursed herself for her latter epiphany.

"Okay. Meet you down there in thirty minutes?" She slowly turned her head to face him.

"I'll make it twenty." Kyle smiled and walked off.

***

Karen wasn't sure if she was playing with fire and whether or not she wanted to get burned as she dipped her toe into the water. She hoped back. "That is really hot."

"It's supposed to be hot." Kyle laughed as he stood from his spot in the hot tub and extended his hand to help Karen descend the steps.

She flinched as her body immersed deeper into the bubbling waters.

Kyle took a deep breath as Karen settled herself opposite of him. She was gorgeous. Smart. Ambitious. His quick perusal of her as she made her way to the hot tub noted that she had body for days and the way her black string bikini painted her frame had him craving for her more and more, but he couldn't let his physical attraction show to her. He needed Karen to see that he wanted her on other levels. He'd keep their conversation sexually neutral as best as he could for as long as he could. "So, did you really enjoy yourself today?"

Karen shot him a daring glare. "You couldn't tell?"

She smiled at him and Kyle fought the urge to rush over to her, snatch her up in his arms, and plant kisses all over her body. He'd done much of that earlier on the beach for the same reason. He'd caught a glimpse of her smiling on his way to greet her. The way she taunted his dreams after their candlelit dinner and kept him tossing and turning with the desire to hold her in his arms all night, he knew that a mere "hello" when he walked up to her wouldn't suffice. He'd hold her as he wanted to do all night long. Seeing Dennis seethe with anger as he cradled Karen in his arms was just an added bonus and a great start to his day with the woman he was becoming so fond of.

"Judging by the way you laughed most of the day, I thought you did, but I just wanna make sure."

A bush rustled nearby shifting Karen's eyes towards it.

Kyle made his way over to Karen's side of the tub and sat next to her. "You're okay. I won't let anyone or anything hurt you." He looked longingly into her eyes.

Karen shook her head. *See, it's stuff like that he says and the way he's looking at me now, like I matter a lot to him, that reminds me that I can't let him get to close to me. You can't get hurt by people if you don't let them in.*

"What are you thinking about?" Kyle asked.

Karen didn't know if it was the heat of the night, the heat from the hot water around her, or Kyle's smoldering stare that had her skin on fire. She cleared her throat and once again subdued the battle of emotions plaguing her thoughts. "Nothing. Just how much this vacation was needed." She closed her eyes and tilted her head back embracing her mainly quiet surroundings.

Kyle scooted closer to her and stared at her relaxed posture. "I really want to kiss your neck."

From the sound of his voice, Karen could tell that Kyle had come dangerously close to her. Close enough to kiss her if he dared to. *Why do I keep finding myself here with him? I can either kiss him and get it over with or kiss him and want more.*

Karen thoughts fumbled as she felt Kyle's knee brush up against her. She didn't need a science kit to know that the heat she felt running rampant through her body was courtesy of Kyle's magnetic presence and not the 104° temperature the tub was set at.

She sat up slowly and opened her eyes only to be mere inches from Kyle's face. In keeping with tradition as of late, her mouth was dry as she locked eyes with him. "Kyle, what are you doing?"

"Trying to decide if I'll take the risk of kissing you and you kneeing me, kissing you hard enough to make you like it, or do nothing but simply continue to stare at you. He inched closer to her face until the breaths from their nostrils intertwined.

She kept her gaze settled on Kyle's. His eyes longed for her to embrace him, for their lips to collide together.

Had the bushes not shook loudly again, Karen would have yielded to the temptation of kissing him, but the constant movement in them rattled her nerves. "I'm just gonna go back up to my room." She accepted the sign being thrown her way and stood up.

Kyle gently grabbed her wrist. "Karen, you don't have to go. I won't try to kiss you again, at least for now. Just stay with me a little while longer."

With Kyle's intense stare at her and the bushes steadily rustling, Karen made her way up the stairs, but looked back over her shoulder at him. "Kyle, I have to go."

Karen ran back to her room. She was glad she freed herself from her attraction to Kyle for the night, but remembered that she'd be walking into a lengthy inquisition when she returned to her room. Melanie was waiting up for her to hear all about her day.

By the time Karen made it to her room, she was out of breath and panting. Not because she high tailed away from Kyle, but she literally hadn't been able to control her breathing since she'd avoided another kiss with him. She was certain it would've been mind-blowing if she'd given in to him.

She found Melanie on the balcony of their room shaking her head.

"What's wrong with you?" Karen's eyebrows lifted as she stared at Melanie.

Melanie wasn't sure if Karen really wanted her to answer that question. Karen and Melanie's room overlooked the hot tub. After just returning from her date with Andrew, Melanie stepped on the balcony to see Karen and Kyle in the hot tub. It was a scene that she eagerly wanted to tease Karen about, but the man in the white t-shirt stooping near a thicket of bushes caught her attention. When he finally stood to walk away before Karen fled from the hot tub, Melanie identified the man. *Does she really wanna know that that creep Dennis was on the other side of that bush spying at her and Kyle when they were in the hot tub?*

9

"I don't want to leave." Karen stared out the balcony door. "I've really been enjoying myself here on the beach."

"It wouldn't matter if you were up in the mountains, as long as Kyle was there, you'd still be enjoying yourself." Melanie laughed as she rolled over and out of the bed. "And why do you continue to set that alarm every day we're here?" Melanie grimaced.

"Because I know it annoys you." Karen stuck out her tongue and laughed.

"You ran already, didn't you?" Melanie asked.

"You know I did."

"And did Kyle join you again this morning?"

"Yes, he did." Karen's smile widened.

"So you're not running away from him anymore?" Melanie laughed.

"No."

"Are you ready to admit out loud that you like him?"

"What?" Karen pretended to be clueless as to

what Melanie was talking about.

"You heard me. You two have been together from sun up 'til sun down these past five days doing only God knows what."

"Doing nothing but talking. Thank you very much." Karen flopped down on the bed.

"Okay, just 'talking' nonstop these past days, but you won't admit to me that he's not as bad as you thought he was and that you actually like him."

"That's because I don't like him." Karen laughed.

"I'm glad you laughed at how silly that lie sounded. Don't forget that you're talking to your best friend. I know you very well."

"Whatever. I may have kind of enjoyed hanging out with him these past days." Karen smiled. "But that doesn't mean that I like him or want something to evolve between us." She wasn't ready to share with Melanie just yet how much she really did like Kyle.

"Yeah, whatever. I'm just glad that Kyle stepped in and captured your attention before Dennis had the chance to."

"You act like Dennis is bad. Like it wouldn't be right if I did talk to him."

"He is and it wouldn't be." Melanie jumped back under the covers.

"You don't even know him, so how can you say that he's bad?"

"First impressions are everything. You've talked about him in passing and how he's been a great friend to you on the job, but to actually meet him in person, he's kind of creepy."

"Creepy? Why would you say that?"

"That whack lie he made up about him and his boys just picking a place on the globe and showing up here, so lame." Melanie laughed.

"I thought it was kind of cute." Karen shrugged her shoulders.

"No, creepy and lame are better words to describe him. Instead of being honest with you about how he showed up here, he lied. That doesn't sit well with me." Melanie still wasn't sure if she should tell Karen that she caught Dennis spying on her. On one hand, she'd want to know if someone was stalking her, but on the other hand, the knowledge could land Karen on TMZ after she tore into Dennis. She decided she'd keep a close eye on him when she could for the time being.

"Oh, whatever. Kyle did the same thing." Karen stood in the balcony door smiling and thinking about Kyle.

"No, that was cute of Kyle. He's been sending you flowers and notes, and then he tracks you down here. He's been consistent and forward with his pursuit of you. Dennis just popping up out of the blue is so random and weird. It just gives me the heebie jeebies thinking about it." Melanie pretended to shake wildly and scratch her arms as if she was trying to wipe off the thoughts of Dennis.

"As usual, you're so dramatic." Karen picked up a pillow from the chair nearby and threw it at Melanie.

Melanie ducked under the covers.

"I'll admit that I never looked at Dennis in a

romantic way before, but every woman at some point wants to and enjoys being adored by a man. And it just so happens that Dennis is handsome and successful, so there was nothing wrong with me enjoying his advances. He seemed genuine to me."

Melanie peeked her head out. "Well, keep believing that if you want to. I'm just glad that Kyle is winning." She ducked under the covers again hoping to avoid another pillow.

Karen smirked and headed onto the balcony to watch the waves wash ashore.

***

"Man, open up the door." Andrew banged on Kyle's door.

"What do you want?"

"Let me in, unless…"

Kyle opened the door and went back to the balcony. He heard the waves crashing at the foot of the shore. He caught a glimpse of Karen sitting on her balcony across the courtyard. She looked so peaceful taking in the scenery.

Andrew peaked into the bathroom, the closet, and under the bed.

Kyle looked in the room to see Andrew snooping. "What are you doing?"

"Checking to see if you're alone."

"You're an idiot." Kyle shook his head.

Andrew stepped onto the balcony. His gaze traveled to where Kyle's was. "So you're a stalker now, hunh? It's bad enough that you made an impromptu trip down here to see her, but now you're hiding out on balconies just stalking her, I mean staring at her? What has she done to you, my brother?" Andrew shook Kyle's shoulders as if trying to loosen Karen's hold on him.

"Nothing. I told you that she's special. She's different. I meet so many women who want me just for my money or the fame they can get being with me, but she's not like that at all. She has her own money. She's smart. Sexy. Beautiful. She's the total package. And ain't you the tortoise calling the hare slow." Kyle laughed.

Andrew's eyebrows furrowed.

"Don't act like you don't understand what I'm saying."

Andrew laughed.

"You talking about me, but you haven't left Melanie's side either since we got here," Kyle said.

"That's different."

"How?"

"She never dissed me the way Karen did you." Andrew laughed. "We just clicked from the beginning. When it's like that, it's right, but if Karen keeps rejecting you the way she does, she may not be the one for you. Besides, training camp will be starting soon, and you have no time to be chasing after a woman. Remember your goal this year is to get a ring, not give a woman a ring."

"Man, shut up." Kyle laughed. "I know that she's putting up a front. She doesn't want to get hurt, but once she gets to know me, she'll let her guard down."

"Bet?"

"Yeah, bet. I know she will."

"Don't be so cocky now. You keep saying that you like her feistiness. That's what might keep you from hooking up with her. Just remember you have a ring to win. And will you stop stalking her already?" Andrew said annoyed.

Kyle moved closer to Andrew towering over him by almost a foot.

Andrew didn't back down from Kyle's defensive stance.

Kyle grabbed Andrew into a headlock, and the two began to playfully wrestle. The curtains hanging at the balcony door fell as the duo's wrestling match rolled back into the room.

Andrew managed to undo himself from Kyle's headlock and pinned Kyle to the floor. "Don't think that because you're a pro athlete you're stronger than me. Remember I taught you everything you know, youngin'."

Kyle laughed and mustered up enough strength to roll over until he had Andrew pinned in a headlock.

The lamp on the nightstand fell to the floor in big pieces.

"Look at what you've done, playing around so much. Fool, let me up." Andrew could barely breathe.

"Nope. Not unless you stop nagging me about Karen."

Andrew nodded his head up and down.

Kyle let Andrew go. Andrew took deep breaths. Kyle jumped to his feet and headed back to the balcony door. Andrew jumped on Kyle's back.

"Sucka! I'mma clown you about her forever." Andrew laughed.

Kyle spun around trying to sling Andrew off his back and all thirty-seven inches of the TV went crashing to the floor. Andrew fell to his feet.

"See what you did? This room is in my name, not yours." Kyle fumed.

"Sorry, man," Andrew said.

They both looked at the mess on the floor before they broke out in laughter.

"Come on, let's just go. It's time to check out anyway. Besides, you can afford to cover the damages."

"You better hope they don't ban me from this hotel or any of their other ones." Kyle shook his head ande grabbed his bags as they left the room.

***

"Mr. Irving, did you enjoy your stay?" The young front desk clerk smiled and leaned forward exposing more of her breasts to Kyle.

Andrew stood by laughing. He whispered to Kyle. "That's why Karen doesn't want you, women constantly throw themselves at you."

Cameras flashed around them.

"You ready for round two? Right here in the lobby?" Kyle threatened.

"Naw, man. I'm cool." Andrew laughed.

"Mr. Irving, housekeeping just phoned from your room that there is extensive damage to major items in the room." The clerk stood up straight with a stern look on her face as the manager appeared next to her to speak to Kyle.

Karen and Melanie arrived at the front desk, and another clerk began to check them out.

"Hola. Enjoyed your stay, senoras?" The clerk asked.

"Yes. I don't want to leave." Karen pouted.

"Here's your card back. Thank you for staying at The Westin, and we do hope that you would come back again." The older woman smiled.

"Most definitely." Karen turned and walked right into Dennis. "Dennis. I'm sorry for bumping into you."

"It's okay." Dennis held Karen at her waist to keep her from falling over.

Kyle noticed the exchange and began ignoring the front desk manager as the manager informed him and Andrew on the expenses for the damages.

"You just seemed to have come from out of nowhere." Melanie tightened her mouth.

Karen readjusted her purse on her arm and patted her hair smooth.

"I checked out already, so I was just headed out to see if my car was here to take me to the airport. You ladies want to ride with me?"

Kyle had his back turned completely towards the clerks and was listening intently to Karen and Dennis's conversation.

"Um, um..." Karen words trailed off as she looked back at Kyle. "Thanks for the offer, but I already have a ride."

Dennis looked over at Kyle. "Oh, I see. Well, I'll see you around the studio on Monday unless I see you again before then." Dennis looked apprehensively at Kyle for a second and then walked off. He pulled out his phone and texted someone.

Kyle smiled.

Andrew took care of the expenses while Kyle stared at Karen.

She walked towards the door to escape the trance he held her in and the many people steadily taking pictures of him.

"So ladies, you all ready to go?" Andrew asked.

"Yes." they said in unison. Melanie looked at Andrew and smiled. Karen looked off into the landscape as she headed to the car.

Cameras flashed as they got into the limo and closed the doors.

"Karen, why are you so far up there? You're practically kissing the partition," Melanie said. They all laughed.

Karen ignored them. She stared at the resort's beautifully manicured landscape until they reached the gate. From then on, she looked at the residential streets of St. Lucia until they reached the airport.

***

Cameras flashed.

Droves of busty women stood by winking and blowing kisses at Kyle.

"Sorry, Mr. Irving. We tried to keep them back," the limo driver said as he opened the door to let them out.

"No problem, I'm used to it." He moved over in his seat and allowed Karen and Melanie to exit before he did.

Karen jumped out and rushed ahead of him, tired of the paparazzi.

"Karen, wait up." Melanie caught up with her. "Why the sudden attitude?"

"Nothing's wrong," Karen replied.

"Yes, it is. Spill the beans."

Karen leaned in to whisper to Melanie. "Okay. I admit it. The morning runs, the brunches, the candlelit dinner, the walks along the beach, these past couple of days with Kyle let me see a different side of him and made me to let my guard down a little. I almost forgot who he was until I saw the clerk at the front desk fawning all over him. And now all of these cameras. I don't want this. I don't want him."

They all walked until they made it to the customs line.

"See, man, I told you that you didn't have a chance with her," Andrew mumbled to Kyle.

"Will you shut up already? I told you I got this." Sweat beads formed on Kyle's forehead and his hands became clammy despite the air conditioning being on blast in the airport.

Kyle stood in line waiting for his passport to be checked. He had overheard Karen's last words. *Was she talking about me? What changed? She seemed so into me these past couple of days.*

They made it through customs with ease and

headed to the terminal to board their plane.

En route to the gate, Melanie excused herself to go to the bathroom.

Kyle stayed behind to chat with her when she came out while Karen and Andrew walked ahead, handed their tickets to the customer service agent, and then boarded the plane.

Karen made it back to her row and struggled to fit her overstuffed carry-on into the overhead bin. She had done some major shopping while she was there.

"Hey, let me help you with that." Dennis jumped up out of his seat from across the aisle.

"Oh, hey, Dennis." Given her attitude over Kyle, she was only able to give him half a smile. "Thanks."

"I guess I'm seeing you again sooner than work on Monday, huh?" He smiled but took note of her melancholy mood.

"Yeah, I guess." Karen took her window seat.

Dennis closed the overhead bin and sat back down in his seat. "I'm just an arm's length away from you." He stretched his arm out and rubbed her shoulder.

She was oblivious to his touch.

He wanted to engage her in a conversation. "So, this whole vacation has been such a coincidence. Me showing up here the same time of year you did and even sitting on the exact plane in the same row with you." He smiled hard, but then frowned. "I hate I didn't see you much while we were here."

"Yeah, I was kind of busy." Karen aimlessly stared at the men putting the luggage in the compartments below outside of the plane.

"Karen—" Dennis was interrupted.

Kyle took the empty seat next to Karen.

She recognized his cologne. It intoxicated her. She turned towards him. "What are you doing? You're sitting in Melanie's seat. Shouldn't you be in first class receiving 'mile high' privileges?" She made air quotes with her hands as she spoke.

Kyle shook his head. "When I saw that you weren't sitting in first class, I decided to switch my seat to sit next to you."

"Well I know your long legs will tire quickly from sitting in these tight rows back here, so why don't you go see if your seat is still available up there." She exhaled loudly.

He leaned in closer. "I don't care about being uncomfortable right now. I'm more concerned if you're okay? Why the sudden change of attitude with me? Did I do something wrong?"

"No. You're just you. I forgot about that for a second, but I've come back to my senses." She turned her head back towards the window.

Dennis smiled, overhearing Karen.

Melanie was coming down the aisle towards them.

"What took you so long?" Karen asked Melanie as she walked up to her row smiling.

Karen turned her head to see where Melanie was headed. "Would you take your seat already?" She cocked her head and blinked rapidly at Melanie. "Kyle, you're in Melanie's seat." She never looked at him but continued staring sternly at Melanie.

"I switched seats with Kyle. I'm sitting in first class with Andrew." Melanie winked at Karen and then rushed off to first class. The flight attendants were prompting everyone to take their seats and buckle up.

"You okay, Karen?" Dennis leaned forward in his seat trying to look across the aisle and past Kyle to get Karen's attention.

Karen was lost in her texting conversation with Melanie and couldn't hear Dennis.

Kyle deepened the bass in his voice. "Yeah, she's okay."

"I wasn't talking to you. I was talking to Karen." Dennis's lips tightened as he turned his body towards Kyle.

Kyle did the same. He focused his eyes on Dennis. "I know who you were talking to, but I said that she's good. I got her." Kyle shifted closer in his seat to Karen as the flight attendant took the passengers through the safety procedures for flying.

Even though his phone should have been off, Dennis had his phone out rapidly texting someone.

Karen sat stiff with her body angled away from Kyle during the entire flight back to Chicago.

Kyle was worried.

10

Karen used the key Melanie gave her to let herself into her best friend's condo. Having keys to each other's places was beneficial to them both, especially since they lived across the hall from each other. The smell of Shea butter and coconut oil permeated the air. Karen followed the scent until she found the source of the aroma and Melanie in her master bathroom taking flexi rods out of her natural hair. The hair moisturizer jar was open and apparently, the coconut oil bottle had tipped over, spilling some of its contents. Karen was used to that combo of smells from Melanie for years, and it was a pleasant contrast to the sporty type of perfumes and scents she preferred.

Karen pulled on one of Melanie's soft, spiral curls. It bounced back into place. "You're going out with him again, aren't you?"

"Yes." Melanie laughed. She continued to pull the rods from her hair.

Karen plopped down on the dark brown tufted ottoman in the massive bathroom.

"What? Do you have a problem with me going out with Andrew?" Melanie stared at the mirror until she made eye contact with Karen.

"No. I mean it's nothing wrong with Andrew. I just thought that maybe you and I could catch a movie tonight."

Melanie laughed. "Awww, don't pout. You can easily have someone to go to the movies with. You just refuse to give him a chance."

"Um, who? If you're talking about Kyle, then that's a negative."

"Yes, I'm talking about him. Over the past week, you've refused to answer his calls and—"

"I know. I just can't. I won't. I don't want that kind of life of being with him. Always on the road, females always up in his face throwing themselves at him. I can't deal with that."

"All the flowers he's sent you. All the cards. All the cryptic tweets on twitter, posts on Instagram and Facebook he says about you, and you aren't smitten by any of that?" Melanie twisted her lips for Karen to see that she didn't believe her.

"He's done more than tweet, Instagram, call, text, and email me. He's been up to my job a few times."

Melanie's eyes widened as she stared into the mirror still picking at her hair. "And what did you do?"

"I told Marge to tell him that I wasn't there." Karen laughed. "Okay, I would be lying if I said I didn't like that stuff and all of the attention he's been giving me, but I know that he's just being over the top to win me over, and then once I let my guard down, he'll change, or rather show who he really is and I'll be left hurt."

"You never know unless you give him a try."

"Remember? I've tried. Never again."

Melanie paused. She wondered if she should rehash Karen's past or just move on. She opted for the latter. "Girl, he's only going to chase after you for so long before he finally decides to stop altogether."

"Well, I hope that's sooner than later. Anywho, enough about me, what's up with you and Andrew? You sure have been spending a lot of time with him this past week since we got back from St. Lucia." Karen cooed.

"Whatever. I just feel so comfortable around him. I honestly enjoy spending time with him." Melanie smiled, twirling her hair.

"Well since you have a hot date, I guess I'll just go for another run by my lonesome." She pouted, dragging her feet to the door with her head down.

"Awww, don't be like that, pumpkin. We can always call Kyle and you two can join us tonight." Melanie buckled over with laughter.

"Bye." Karen slammed the door to Melanie's apartment.

She crossed the hall and entered her condo. She took her time putting on her running gear before she headed to the trail.

***

The weather was perfect for running. Although

August was the hottest month in Chicago, the sun had just set, and the soft, summer breeze proved to be perfect company for Karen and her sweat.

She turned on her running playlist and stretched. She extended her arms straight up as if she was trying to reach the sky. Next, she squatted low and rocked from side to side stretching her inner thighs. She was preparing her body to run until thoughts of Kyle no longer existed in her head. She stood up straight and took off running. Looking ahead, she noticed an all too familiar frame. She wondered if she should turn around and run the other way, but since they lived in the same city, their paths would cross eventually. Especially considering she would be covering more of the Bulls games once the season started. She figured that she might as well go ahead and get this final "I don't want you" speech out of the way.

She ran until she reached him. He stood there smiling and jogging in place waiting for her.

Staring at her the way her father used to look at her mother, he handed her a colorful bouquet of flowers.

She tried to hide her smile. "Flowers for me? How did you know I would be here?"

"I didn't. I just took a chance. I haven't been able to run in the mornings since training camp started. You haven't responded to any of my messages or answered my calls. I really wanted to see you and I know you love to run, so I told myself that I would just come out here every evening hoping you get inspired to run, and I would catch you."

"Oh really?"

Kyle smiled, looking at the surprise in Karen's eyes. "I actually came out here earlier, and I didn't see you, but then I was at home looking at some practice footage, and I had this gut feeling to come out here tonight. I'm glad I listened to my gut." He smiled at her as he rocked from his heels to his toes.

Karen's cheeks grew warm. "And you just happened to have these laying around the house?"

He laughed. "No, there's a small flower shop in the lobby of my building. I got them from there."

"Thanks."

"Why haven't you returned any of my calls or responded to any of my texts?"

"I've been really busy."

"You've been that busy for a week where you haven't been able to answer my calls or even come to the front desk when I come to your job?"

"Look, um..."

"Before you say it...I know it's my fault for the reputation that I have, but that is my past. Basketball is all I've ever wanted to do. I'm not like the average basketball player or pro athlete nowadays. Yeah, I messed around with quite a few women when I first got in the league, but that's not me anymore. I've slowed down. I've changed."

"Oh really? What about the woman at the front desk in St. Lucia all over you? Or the women at the airport when we got out of the car?" Karen pressed her lips together. "I know that happens to you everywhere you go. And what about all the cameras and paparazzi constantly following you for the scoop on your life? I wouldn't want our relationship to be the constant talk of the town."

"But you're a celebrity, too."

"Yeah, that's different, Kyle. When my show is over and the cameras go off, I go back to my regular life. But you're always in the spotlight."

"I can't ignore or won't change who I am. I like you. You're not some video vixen that I want to just smash and be done with. I mean, I really like you."

Karen looked down at her running shoes trying to avoid Kyle's stare.

"I thought that we really connected in St. Lucia. We were together practically day in and day out. Running along the beach, midnight walks along the shore, holding hands. We shared a lot with each other. I feel like I really got to know you, the real you, and I like you. I care about you."

Karen smiled. "Yeah, I learned that you are a great guy, but..."

"But what?"

"I just have to stick to what I know. When I first became a sports anchor, I tried dating a celebrity baseball player. He wined and dined me, told me I was different from any other woman he dated, but within the first two weeks I found out that he had a wife."

Kyle coughed, trying to clear his throat.

"Not so shocking to you, hunh? I guess because you know how you all can be."

Kyle shook his head. "Karen, not all of us are deceiving."

"Mmph. I told myself that I wouldn't be a fool

again for a man, but then a year later there was an NFL player who pursued me. He seemed to have it all together and so I tried to give him a chance, but then I look up to find out that he has a baby mama that he lived with and crazy exes stalking me and showing up at my job. I gave him a chance. I fell in love with him, but after that, I knew that I just couldn't be with a professional sports player or celebrity for that matter. I guess you all have too much temptation to resist or turn down."

"But Karen, all male celebrities aren't like that." Kyle huffed. "Any man could've did you like that."

"But I don't get approached by the average man."

"That's because you're not average." Kyle smiled.

"Whatever. No brownie points for you." Karen laughed, but immediately switched back to being serious to continue her tirade. "You said it yourself. When you first got in the game, you did all of that."

"I was young. I practically got drafted out of high school. That was the life that I thought I was supposed to live, but I'm a grown man now. As I've gotten older, I've decided that those aren't the ways that I want, and I honestly have changed."

Karen rested her body weight on one leg and folded her arms across her chest. "So you don't think that anything from your past could possibly come back and haunt you? Us?"

"I mean, I can't say that it won't, but I know I'm a different and better man today. Within these last few years, I know I haven't done anything that would make you want to run away from me. Just give me a chance."

"Kyle, I… I need more time to think about it." She wiped sweat beads from her forehead.

"I can respect that. Will you at least take the flowers?"

"Oh yeah. Thanks." Karen smiled, took the bouquet from Kyle, and buried her face behind it. "They're pretty, just like all the other ones you've sent."

"Can I walk you home?"

"I'm not done running."

"So you're gonna run with that heavy bouquet?" Kyle chuckled.

"Yes." Karen laughed. "The extra weight will amp up my workout."

Kyle shook his head at her as his lips curved wryly. "Well, can I run with you then?"

She smiled. "I don't own Lakeshore Drive so I can't tell you that you can't run out here, but I'd prefer to run by myself tonight. Remember, I have some things to think about."

"Yes, you do. Well, have a good night. Can you at least text or call me and let me know when you make it back home?"

"Okay, I guess."

"Good night, beautiful."

Karen waved at him. She ran away smiling, trying to further distance herself from his charm.

***

Andrew held Melanie as close to him as he

possibly could.

She tilted her head back and allowed the soft, summer breeze to flow through her hair and caress her neck.

He smiled, gazing at her. "What are you thinking about?"

With their bodies closely knit, they continued to sway to the soulful jazz playing through the loud speakers at Millennium Park.

"Nothing much. Just how beautiful it is out here tonight." She lifted her head to stare into his eyes. "And how comfortable I feel with you."

Her eyes had him in a trance.

"Andrew?"

"Oh, I'm sorry. I just get lost in your eyes every time I look into them. Did I tell you how familiar they are to me?"

Melanie furrowed her eyebrows. "Yeah, often, which is starting to make me wonder if I remind you of an ex that you're not over."

Andrew laughed. "Nothing like that. I won't bring it up again."

"Good. Why are you looking like that?"

"Like what?" Andrew laughed.

"All starry-eyed?"

"I was just thinking that at first I wanted Kyle to sign with the Clippers because then it would mean that I would spend more time in L.A., in the sun year round, but I'm glad we ended up here in Chicago, with you." He pecked at her lips.

"So do you follow him to every city that he plays in?"

"Yes and no. I don't necessarily follow him as if I don't have a life, but since he is my most valuable client I choose to be near or in the city that he's playing in. Not to mention he's my best friend, and we have been since kindergarten. We're like brothers. Our parents even raised us to be that way. I am my brother's keeper so I want to protect him from all the snakes in the entertainment industry and even the females who try to get with him just for his money or try to trap him by getting pregnant by him just to get money. You know, gold diggers."

"Yeah and that's why Karen is so scared to give him a chance, because of all of this stuff that happens to celebrities."

"Yeah, but I don't want to talk about them anymore. I want to talk about us."

Melanie batted her eyes and smiled.

11

The flowers Kyle gave Karen on her run was the continuance of him melting her heart and etching his name on it. They talked to each other every free moment of the day from that point on.

When he wasn't in practice and she wasn't at work taping, they were either at each other's places wrapped in each other's arms, zoning out to old school music, and soaking in each other's presence or watching film from some of Kyle's old games.

"So, you think you have my game figured out, hunh?" He threw popcorn at her as they sat on the floor with playbooks sprawled out in front of them.

"Yes." She gathered the kernels and threw them back at him. "I should see if I could get on the coaching staff of the Bulls. With me as your personal coach, you all would definitely win the championship this year." Her smile brightened the dimly lit room.

"Well I don't think you'll be on the staff anytime soon, but with you by my side as my woman, I feel like I've won several championships already."

"Your woman?"

"Don't raise your eyebrows at me. Yeah, I said it... My woman."

Kyle gathered himself on his hands and knees and crawled over to Karen to kiss her soft lips.

She wanted to pull away from him, but that stare of his made her gladly oblige him.

He slowly eased her back flat on the floor and covered her body with his. He kissed her neck as she moaned and wiggled underneath him. He braced himself on his elbows and glowered at her.

She lifted her head off the floor trying to kiss him, but he pulled back from her.

Her eyebrows furrowed. "What's wrong?"

"Nothing. I just want to stare at you."

She made funny faces and allowed him to stare at her for a while before she tried to kiss him again.

He pulled back from her again.

"Okay, Kyle, what's up?" She pushed him off her.

He rolled onto his side, propping his smooth, bald head on his hand as he stared at her sitting Indian style in front of him with a perturbed look on her face.

"Why do you think something is wrong with me?" He smirked.

"Because you kept pulling back from me when I tried to kiss you. Every time we're kissing, passionately might I add, you stop us from doing you know what..." Karen looked down and played with the fibers of her shaggy carpet. She normally didn't rush to be so intimate with a man. They didn't have to have sex, but she wondered why Kyle never gave in to do so.

He smiled at her before he spoke. "Karen, we've only been seeing each other for a month."

"Five weeks if you count St. Lucia."

Kyle laughed. "Okay, five weeks. I want something serious with you and I want you to know that, so I'm not going there with you until I know for sure that you're ready, and you're not just being hot in the pants."

Karen laughed and hit Kyle with a throw pillow she grabbed from the couch.

He laughed and grabbed the pillow pulling her into him. He fell back on his back and positioned her next to him, resting her head in the crook of his arm. He held her tightly with his free arm.

"Who Can I Run To?" by Xscape played softly in the background. They let the music fill the air for a while.

Kyle cleared his throat before speaking again. "Karen?"

"Yeah." She was dozing off.

"I love you."

Her eyes popped open. She sat up to look him in the eyes, but he held her tightly to him. He turned on his side so that they could see each other eye to eye.

"What did you say?" Her mouth was completely dry.

"You heard me. I love you."

"But Kyle, it's only been five weeks like you said. You can't be. You just can't."

He could feel her heart beating fast against his

chest. She tried to pull away from him, but he held on tightly to her. He saw the look of fear in her eyes before his eyes calmed her.

"It's not about time with us. I knew from the moment I met you running that first day that there was something special about you. It's taken five weeks for my brain to catch up to what my heart knew from day one."

Karen tried to pull back from him again, but he kept a tight hold of her.

"Why are you still trying to run from me?"

"Because, you can't say that you love someone after only knowing them for five weeks, six if you count that week I avoided you." She laughed, trying to mask her nervousness.

"So, you don't believe in love at first sight?" Kyle smiled.

"The little girl in me wants to, but…"

"But what?"

"No, I don't."

Kyle could tell from the tremble in her voice that she wasn't convinced of her answer, and neither was he.

"I admit that I didn't at first, but I'm a believer now. It doesn't take years or a lifetime to realize that you've met the one you want to spend the rest of your life with. I don't care what you say, I know that I love you, Karen Charice Roberts." He pecked at her lips.

She pulled back from him. Her eyes were glossy. She mumbled, "I won't say the same right now."

"I didn't ask you too. I just wanted you to know

how I feel, and I'll continue to show you that I do until you feel it enough to realize that you love me."

"So, you're just gonna make me fall in love with you, hunh?" She smiled at him.

"I think I've already done that. I'm just gonna have to make you say it." He winked.

12

"I like that blazer on you. Break a leg. I know you will do great as usual." Marge winked.

"Thanks, Marge." Karen buttoned her blazer, smoothed her skirt, and headed to the set.

The gossip segment that came on late night was still taping their session. Karen had to stand off the set and wait for production to wrap up.

She made light conversation with an assistant until a name mentioned by the chatty gossip show host caught her attention.

"Just when we thought that we had met our quota for celebrity scandal for the year, Kyle Irving proved us wrong. We have Mercedes Silva here with us. Welcome."

"Thank you." The Brazilian beauty gave a brief smile.

"So you're claiming that Kyle Irving is the father of your daughter?" Chatty Cathy sipped her tea.

"Yes."

"Why wait to come forward now? Why not when you were pregnant? I mean, I really want to know."

Mercedes hesitated before she spoke, and when she finally did, she made sure that she spoke slowly to be understood through her thick accent. "Well, I wasn't going to come forward and say anything, but once a common friend of ours realized that my daughter was his, she leaked the story to several tabloids. My Instagram, twitter, and Facebook accounts have been swamped with mean comments from his fans. I deactivated my accounts to avoid all of that drama, but then the media started showing up at my house, my family's houses, following me around town harassing me, so I thought I might as well tell it rather than let the lies continue to spread."

"Honey, I keep up with the tabloids and blogs, I'm the queen of them." Cathy, the chatty host, threw her head back and tossed her layered extensions over her shoulder. "I haven't read anything about this story, but you're saying that you've been hounded?"

"It may not have been the most popular blogs or tabloids, but there were a lot of attacks on me to the point where I felt I just had to come forth and tell my story."

"Were you all in a relationship?"

"We weren't necessarily in a relationship."

"So what was it? Just a friend with benefits?"

Mercedes eyes widened as she cocked her head back. "I'm not a groupie or a gold digger. It's not like I sought him out. It was the other way around."

Cathy leaned closer to Mercedes. "Do tell."

"Like I said, we have, 'had', a mutual friend."

"Hold on, why did you say 'had' like that?"

"Because she was the one who sold the story to

the tabloids when she learned that my daughter wasn't my ex's that I had been with off and on with for the past seven years."

"How did this 'friend' know that?"

"Because my ex is Brazilian as well, and anyone can tell that my daughter has a lot of African American in her. The older she gets, the more she looks like Kyle. My ex saw that, and he got a paternity test for my daughter. When the results came back that she wasn't his, he left. Well, once my 'friend' found out why my ex left, she automatically knew my daughter was Kyle's."

Cathy looked into the camera. "This is getting good, America." She turned her attention back towards Mercedes. "So you say you all weren't in a relationship, but you weren't just a booty call. So what was it really?"

Mercedes breathed deeply hoping to find the right words to say. "Right, not technically a relationship. I guess you could say we were friends. He treated me in a way where I let my guard down and we were intimate soon and often."

"Mmhh, so have you spoken to him at all, or did you just run straight to the media? Are you seeking child support?"

Mercedes shifted in her seat. "Like I said, I'm just trying to clear my name. Maybe I should have tried to settle things with him first, but I didn't. I'm not going after him for child support, but it would be nice if he were willing to help raise her."

Karen barely breathed as she continued to listen to the segment. She didn't want to miss a thing that was being said.

"So you're saying that he may not be aware that your daughter is his?"

"Yes, that may be the case."

Cathy looked into the camera. "Well, Kyle Irving, I guess you just found out here on 'Mountaintop Hour' that you may have a child. You might want to round up your legal team and accountants for this one." She turned to face Mercedes again. "Well, it was nice to meet you, Mercedes, and just know that I will be commenting on this story as new information unfolds. Hey, I might even have you all back on the show as one big happy family, you never know."

Mercedes gave a half-hearted smile.

"Until next time America, deuces." Cathy held the universal peace sign near her face.

"And cut."

Cathy's production team continued to wrap up the segment and make way for Karen's team to set up the set for her segment.

Karen watched as Mercedes finally left the stage. She seemed shaken. Not the confident, gold-digging-baby-momma type.

Should I say something to her? Get more details about what really happened between her and Kyle? No! I would look crazy. He and I have only been together for a little over a month. Well, technically he says I'm his woman, but I'm not claiming him just yet...but he told me he loves me, and I know that I...

Mercedes walked past Karen and gave her a friendly grin as she was ushered to her green room.

Karen could see why Kyle would want Mercedes.

She was beautiful. Long, layered hair, stacked hour-glass figure, clear-beautiful skin, and she smelled of the lightest lavender possible. Kind of like the smell of the bottle of perfume Kyle bought for her because, although he loved the sporty fragrances she wore, he wanted her to wear that scent sometimes, too.

A headache surfaced at Karen's temples. *Once again, I was stupid to think that I could have a happily ever after with a pro player.*

Karen didn't have time to sulk just yet. She had a sports segment to render to her nearly thirty million viewers that tuned in weekly for her take on sports.

She had to be her best on camera because even though she was a great basketball player, her father always praised her on her basketball I.Q. and how she could really break the game down and analyze players. Instead of focusing on playing basketball in college, she focused on journalism with an emphasis in sports so that she could honor her father and make him proud. She brought her thoughts back to the broadcast for the day.

Dennis was her guest co-host for the segment. He walked on stage smiling.

She put on her game face and met him on the stage.

***

Andrew shook his head. He couldn't believe how fast bad news spread. It seemed like just yesterday Kyle was in the headlines for signing with the Chicago Bulls and being praised for being who the team needed to win their seventh NBA title, but today he checked social media to find out that there is some Brazilian woman claiming that Kyle fathered her child and Chatty Cathy of all people covered the breaking story. He would have to figure out a way quick and in a hurry to get Kyle out of this debacle before the season started.

***

"Man, I sure am glad that you play better than you look." The Bulls small forward ragged on Kyle.

"Whatever, man. Just because I am the new guy on this team doesn't mean that I'm a rookie and y'all can treat me any kind of way." Kyle laughed and popped a few of his teammates with his towel.

There was thunderous laughter in the locker room as many of them ran from him avoiding his hits.

The players grabbed their gym bags and left the locker room and headed down the corridor that led to the players parking cove.

"Man, I can't wait for the season opener on Friday night. It's going to be mad crazy. You've never experienced this kind of electricity until you've been a Chicago Bulls on the season opening night." The point guard pretended to shine Kyle's bald head like a pair of shoes as he walked past him and popped the lock to his Ferrari.

Everyone left except for Kyle. He stood there trying to respond to the buzzing of his phone. It was Andrew. Before he could even send a response, Andrew appeared out of the shadows of the tunnel.

"Man, if it ain't one thing with you, it's another." Andrew shook his head.

Kyle was confused. "What do you mean? Everything's good. The season is about to start. We know we're about to go on a winning streak with yo' boy, me being added to the team." Kyle laughed. "I'm just excited for this season and I got my girl on my side. Winning." Kyle bounced his shoulders as if he was dancing.

"Uh, I don't know about that. I'm pretty sure if she saw any of what I saw then she won't be your girl any longer."

"You're trippin'. What are you talking about?"

"What am I talking about? What am I talking about? Here, you tell me." Andrew gave his phone to Kyle with the latest blog coverage of Mercedes on the screen.

Kyle's eyes widened as he rubbed his goatee. He read the different headlines and comments on the blogs about him. He couldn't believe a woman was claiming to have his daughter, but all he could think about was what Karen would think of it. He knew he needed to get to her as soon as possible to explain the situation. He threw his bag in the backseat and was about to jump in the driver's seat when Andrew pulled at his arm.

"Man, where are you going?"

"I need to go talk to Karen." Kyle tried to get in his car.

Andrew tugged Kyle's elbow again. "No, you need to handle this situation. You can talk to Karen at a later time. Do you even know this chick? Let me see what she said her name is... Mercedes Silva. Do you know her?"

Kyle was eager to say no until he stopped to think about the woman he had a summer fling with some years back. It was nothing serious between them, but he did remember that it was pretty serious between the sheets. He leaned back against his car recalling that he met her through a mutual friend. He was grateful for that hookup. He couldn't get enough of Mercedes at that time because he had the best sex with her since he had turned pro. After her, he decided that he wanted to be more of a one woman man. He determined that she would be the last woman he would bed so quickly before really getting to know her.

"Kyle, Kyle man do you hear me?"

"Hunh, hunh?"

"I've been talking to you for the last few minutes and you haven't paid attention to anything I've said. You don't have time to worry about what Karen thinks. You have to get this situation under control. You're barely on the team, the season hasn't even started, and you already have a scandal. We don't need anything to make management rethink that contract they just gave you."

"Man, players have domestic issues all the time. I don't think they will get rid of me just because of this, over something that might not even be true. Nah, that's not going to happen." Kyle scratched his bald head. "I don't get it. She didn't seem bitter when I ended things with her."

"How do you know?"

"I know because she told me 'thank you.' Said that it would give her the chance to work on her relationship with the dude she had been dealing with off and on for years. So I don't get why she would come forth now claiming I'm the father when I know she had a guy."

"Well, let me handle this one point at a time."

Kyle continued leaning on his car rubbing his chin.

"Contrary to your belief, players can't just do any and everything and get away with it. You see how these different leagues are cracking down on the things that these players do because the public is expecting them to make an example of the troubling situation. You can't just father a child and not pay child support or not do anything for that child and think that it won't tarnish your reputation with the public or affect your standing with the team. Not to mention all the endorsements you have might be snatched away from you. You're so close to fulfilling your career goals to allow them to be ruined by some woman saying that you fathered her child, and you're not there or haven't been around for her. Deadbeat fathers don't make good sports drink models."

"Look, man, I hear you and believe it or not, I am concerned about my reputation with the public and my standing with the organization. However, I have to go and see Karen and try to explain it to her. I have to do it now. She already had negative impressions of pro athletes, so I have to go do recon with her now." Kyle's eyes pleaded for Andrew's understanding.

"You do know that if you slept with her and as much as you say you did, there's always the possibility that the girl is yours."

"Yeah I know that, but I have to go to Karen now."

"Well, I see there is no stopping you. Go ahead, man. I'll try to reach out to this Mercedes woman and see if there's some way we can get her to stop talking to the media. See if we can try to resolve this issue more discreetly. We definitely have to get a paternity test done as soon as possible."

"Thanks, bro."

Kyle and Andrew were so engrossed in their conversation that they didn't even notice the group of photographers heading in their direction with two sassy pregnant women leading the pack.

The women allowed the cameras to roll before they began to speak. Porsha spoke first. "Hey, Kyle. You remember me?" She licked her lips and turned around exposing her noticeably ample butt.

Kyle looked down for a moment in confusion before he looked at her face. "What? Who are you?"

"Awww, so now you act like you don't know me. You weren't acting funny those nights we were going at it like wild animals for hours and hours and hours." She licked her lips again and tried to lean in to kiss him, but he stepped back from her.

The cameramen made sure they tracked every movement between the two.

Unique spoke next. "Yeah, Kyle, you were with her one week and then with me the next." Unique's almond colored hands framed her body from her perky breasts to her curvy hips.

"Man, what the hell? Get out of my face with this. I don't know either one of you." Kyle's voice vibrated in the air.

A reporter shoved a microphone into Kyle's face. "So you're saying that you don't know these two ladies? These two pregnant ladies?"

"You heard me. I don't know them. I don't care if they are pregnant, I don't know them. I've never seen them before." Kyle's eyes narrowed in on the cameraman.

"You just spent the last five years in our hometown, Miami. Oh, you know us. You know us very well."

Andrew could tell by Kyle's puffed up chest and the rapid blinking of his eyes that he was getting dangerously frustrated. He didn't know how Kyle would react in front of the cameras if the women and reporters continued to badger him, so he stepped in between Kyle and the women.

The women rolled their eyes at him, sizing him up from top to bottom.

"Okay, ladies and gentlemen, this circus is over. Please move out the way so that my client can leave."

None of them moved, but instead tried to advance closer to Kyle as he entered his car.

The women grabbed the car door trying to keep Andrew and Kyle from closing it, but Andrew was strong enough to hold them back as Kyle jumped in and sped off en route to Karen's condo.

***

Kyle made it to Karen's building faster than he ever had before. He jumped out of the car and practically threw his keys at the valet as he rushed through the glass doors.

"Hi, Mr. Irving." Lonnie, the doorman, frowned.

"Hi, Lonnie. How are you?" Kyle didn't even look at Lonnie as he spoke and walked past the desk headed to the elevators.

"Mr. Irving?" Lonnie called him forcefully.

"What, Lonnie? Now is not a good time."

"If you would slow down, sir, I could save you the trouble of trying to enter her code for the elevator. It won't work."

"Hunh?" Kyle looked puzzled.

"It won't work, sir."

"Yes, it will." Kyle practically stomped over to the elevator and entered the code Karen gave him the night he told her he loved her.

He input the code several times, but the mirrored doors never opened. He stood there for quite some time staring at the creases in his forehead before he made his way back over to Lonnie.

"Lonnie, why won't the code work?" His shoulders slumped.

"I'm sorry, sir, but Ms. Roberts changed the code the moment she got home this evening."

"Well, can't you give it to me?"

"I'm sorry, sir, I can't."

Kyle pulled out his phone and texted Karen several messages. He waited, but she never responded.

He dialed her number, but it kept going straight to voicemail. He decided to leave her a message. "Karen, let's talk about this. Let me explain. Please, baby, pick up the phone when I call again or call me back. I love you and you know I do."

Lonnie stood by sorting through mail pretending not to hear Kyle's pleas.

"Lonnie, can you call up to her place for me?" He shoved his phone back in its holster.

"Sir..."

"Look, I'm not trying to get you in trouble, Lonnie. I just really need to talk to her right now."

Lonnie hated to see one of his favorite basketball players in such despair, plus he knew how much Kyle did care about Karen and how crazy Karen was about him. He handed Kyle the receiver.

Karen's house phone rang. She picked it up believing it was Lonnie downstairs. "Yes, Lonnie. How can I help you?" She smiled.

"Karen, would you let me up or—"

Karen hung up the phone.

Kyle tried calling her back several times on Lonnie's line, but she never answered again.

"Sorry, sir," Lonnie said to Kyle.

"You tried to help me, Lonnie. Thank you." Kyle shoved his hands in his pocket and walked out of the building with his head low.

***

Melanie didn't even bother to knock. She used the key Karen had given her to let herself in. She knew where she would find Karen—on the floor in front of her flat screen TV.

Karen sat there with a gallon of Baskin-Robbins Cookies and Cream ice cream, stuffing one spoonful after another into her mouth.

Karen stared at the replay of the segment that she had witnessed in-person earlier. The new footage of two more women saying that Kyle was the father of their babies added more droplets of rain to the downpour of emotions that she had experienced earlier on the set.

Nothing from my past within the past few years should come back to haunt me or threaten what could become of us. Kyle's words rang in her head. "Such a liar," she mumbled as she looked up and noticed Melanie taking away her comfort. She tried to hold on to it, but Melanie's grip was strong. She released the ice cream.

Karen gathered enough strength to roll herself onto the couch and flop one of the throw pillows on top of her head.

Melanie came back from the kitchen and snatched the pillow from Karen's head. She sat next to Karen on the edge of the couch.

"I can't believe that I fell for it. I open my heart, and I allowed him to walk into it, but I guess he decided to walk all over it."

"Karen, you two were only dating for a little over a month. You think that was really love? It's not like you've been in love with him for years and just finding out about these women and his alleged children."

Karen bucked her head and looked at Melanie. "You've only been talking to Andrew for a month and you seem to walk around here with your head in the clouds as if you're totally in love with him."

"Touché. That's true, but I think there's still a difference between us. Andrew and I recognized our chemistry from the beginning. It's like we were meant to be together." Melanie smiled. "You resisted Kyle for a while before he wore you down, won you over. Maybe it isn't as strong as you want it to be." Melanie knew her words may have sounded harsh to Karen, but it was too late to take them back.

Karen shot Melanie an incredulous look. "Kyle had to work for my attention. You just threw yours at Andrew." Karen saw the hurt look in Melanie's eyes. "I'm sorry, Mel. I didn't mean it the way it sounded."

"I'm sorry, too. I know how I feel about Andrew, and you know how you feel about Kyle and that's all that matters."

They smiled at each other before getting back to the topic at hand.

"Yes, I resisted him at first, but that's only because I knew that I would fall for him hard if I gave him the chance. I wasn't ready to risk my heart being broken, but his charm and that look in his eyes tore down the fortress I had built around my heart."

Karen huffed and snatched her pillow back from Melanie. "He didn't even care to tell me that he slept with so many women in the past couple of years that he might have several baby mommas out there. You and I haven't really been successful in the 'love' department, so how do we really know what it is to love someone or really be loved by them?"

Melanie paused for a moment weighing Karen's words. "Well, honey, you did say that was one of the reasons you didn't want to mess with pro-athletes or celebrities for that matter in the first place. And even though we haven't been successful with it before, that doesn't mean that we can't recognize it when it's real and in our faces. We should, right?" Melanie wondered if she really knew what love was, but didn't think that it was wise to share her doubts with Karen at that time.

"Yes, I said that I didn't want to date him, but don't forget that you encouraged me to give him a chance. I let my guard down with him. I felt like I was getting to know the true him. I, I..." Karen buried her face in her hands to hide her tears.

"Karen, the true him is that he is a great guy with a past. You might not see a bright side to this but at least you found out about this during the 'puppy dog' stage of love and not years down the road where you're truly in love with him and you have to deal with it as his wife and the mother of his children."

"Who said that I'm not already really in love with him?" Karen couldn't believe that she let that slip out.

Melanie smiled. Despite her earlier statements, she knew Karen loved Kyle. She just wouldn't explore it at that point.

Karen was grateful that Melanie didn't call her out on her admission of Kyle. That was the first time she had said it out loud, admitted it to herself. "And you're right. I don't see a bright side to this."

Karen shifted on the couch to face Melanie. "Would you believe that I sat there as this Mercedes chick gave her version of what happened between her and Kyle? I had to look at how beautiful she is. I kept thinking that what she was saying had to be true because any man would easily fall for her."

"Karen, you're beautiful, too. So what does her beauty have to do with anything?"

Karen shrugged her shoulders. "I don't know where that came from. Just a thought, but anyway, she smiled as she walked past me. She didn't seem like the gold-digging type. I kinda believe her."

"Just because she smiled at you doesn't mean that she's trustworthy. Have you even talked to Kyle yet?"

"No, and I'm not going to. I'm not going to give him another moment of my time." Karen reclined on the couch and folded her arms at her chest.

"If you have this connection, this chemistry with him that you say you've had since St. Lucia, then you should be willing to at least hear him out."

"Nope." Karen pouted. "Well enough of this moping and sulking. I'm just going to lace up and run this off." Karen patted her cheeks dry.

"What?"

"You heard me. I'm about to run this off. Running is my antidote."

13

The alarm buzzed. Karen flew from under the covers to turn it off.

The sunlight peeking through her shades hurt her eyes and seemed to agitate the pounding in her head. She stretched and immediately patted her eyes. Just as she suspected, they were puffy from crying all night long. With Melanie taking all of her ice cream, she had nothing but her tears to console her the rest of last night after her run.

She felt like her heart had left her body the night before, and she was now just a shell of a person, but she knew she needed to get out of bed and get herself together for the day. TV personalities had no business looking like they had hangovers.

Although her short-lived romance with Kyle was far more intense than the ones she had with the baseball player, NFL player, or any other man for that matter, she knew, hoped, that in time, she would get over Kyle.

She walked to her bathroom and turned the multiple showerheads on. She wanted it hot and steamy, wishing the steam would open her pores and her sadness and hurt would ooze out and wash down the drain.

She headed over to her sink and braced herself on the counter sighing and thinking of the day ahead of her. She rationalized that she would be so busy at work prepping for her upcoming segments and writing some articles for a few different publications that she wouldn't even have time to think about Kyle and his three baby mommas.

Karen looked at her phone and noticed that she had twenty unread text messages from Kyle. She didn't even bother to read them. Instead, she selected all of them and swiftly pressed delete before her heart betrayed her and encouraged her to read them. She was about to put the phone down when she noticed that her voicemail alert signaled her that she had twenty-five messages from him. She didn't want to hear the messages either because she didn't want to hear the deep bass in his voice that always did something to her, drew her closer to him. She deleted them all, stripped down to nothing, then jumped in the shower.

***

"Good morning, Marge. How are you doing?" Karen tried to inject joy into her voice.

"I would be doing fine if my allergies weren't acting up and I didn't have to inhale all of these different flowers." Marge sneezed. "I mean, one bouquet should be enough for a man to tell a woman how he really feels, but sending twenty bouquets plus three different Edible Arrangements screams 'I love you and you better know it.'"

"Oh, how sweet. Your husband sent you all of these flowers?" Karen admired the assorted array of flowers and colors.

"Once again, they're not for me. They're for you." Marge winked at Karen.

"For me?" Karen held her breath as she reached for a card from one of the bouquets. She scanned it to see Kyle's name. She snarled, then threw the card in the trash can near her feet and walked towards her desk.

Marge sat inquisitively, taking in Karen's changing faces. "Why'd you do that?"

"Because they're from Kyle."

"All the more reason why I would think you would be so much more excited about them than you are."

"Well, I'm not," Karen growled. "You can have them if you like."

"You want to give me your flowers from Kyle? You adore and stare at the bouquet he sends daily, so why would you want to give me these now? You've snarled at me when I've asked for them before, but now you're doing it looking at them. Why the sour face, kiddo?" Marge sneezed repeatedly.

"Nothing's wrong. Don't worry about it." Karen's eyebrows raised as she turned and stared at Marge who was still sneezing and her eyes were watery. "Allergies? But how can you be allergic to flowers when you're in your garden practically year-round?"

"I'm not allergic to them. It's just so many different ones in this space and plus there's something the florist must've sprayed on them that's giving me the flux. They're beautiful, but too much for my nostrils right now." Marge sneezed again. "Getting back to that sour face of yours, I know there's something wrong with you. For the past month since you've been spending day and night with Kyle Irving, you've come in here every day so excited and extra chummy. But today, there's something different about you. Come on. Let it all out. You know you'll feel better after you tell old Marge." She grabbed tissues from her desk before she went to Karen's desk.

"I'm telling you, there's nothing wrong with me." Karen could tell that Marge wasn't buying the lie she was trying to sell her. "Marge, I promise that I'm fine. I just didn't get enough sleep last night, that's all."

"I've seen you when you haven't had enough sleep, and those bags under your eyes aren't it. But this here," Marge grabbed Karen by the chin and looked into her gloomy eyes, "the sadness behind those eyes are saying something different. I'll leave it alone for now, but you know as well as I do that I'll get it out of you before the day is over. Speaking of Kyle, he's called at least five times for you, so I'll just go back over to my desk while you sit at yours twirling your hair with starry eyes as you talk to him."

"We weren't speaking of him when you brought him up, and we won't be talking about him ever again. So if he calls back, will you please tell him to stop calling me, and you don't have to be polite about it."

"Oh, so he's who has you so sad this morning." Marge perked up.

"I'm not sad. See, I'm smiling." Karen manufactured a smile.

"Honey, that smile is about as fake as those flowers on the wallpaper in the women's bathroom."

"I don't want to talk about it now, Marge."

"Well, honey, he sent you all these bouquets, except for that other one over there. It's a lovely arrangement, but not like the others. I think it might have come from a different florist. You're sad and don't want to talk to or about him, but judging by the calls and all of these flowers, clearly he wants to talk to you."

Karen grabbed the bouquet of flowers that Marge was holding and threw them away. She wiped her hands of water from the flowers as if she was cleaning them of Kyle. She then went over to pick up the beautiful vase of the flowers that Marge had pointed out were different.

She wasn't much into flowers, but they were so pretty that she absentmindedly stuck her nose in them until she remembered the last time she did that and who they were from. She pulled her face from them immediately and headed to the trash can with them when she noticed that the card in them didn't match the cards in the other bouquets. She picked it up and read it. *Hi, Karen. Just thinking of you. We didn't get the chance to spend much time together in*

St. Lucia, but hopefully we can catch up soon. I hope to hear from you soon. She smiled.

She could really use another friend. She knew she had Melanie, but Melanie at times seemed to be on Kyle's side. She wanted to enjoy herself free of "Kyle" thoughts and conversations, but then again, maybe Dennis could give her a male perspective of what was going on with her and Kyle. At any rate, he could be another shoulder to lean on, if needed.

She woke up that morning acting as if everything was okay and that she would be easily able to get over Kyle, but at that very moment looking at all the flowers Kyle had sent her, her heart hurt. It had been a short romance with him, but it seemed like an eternity. The conversations between them flowed smoothly. She mulled over how comfortable she had felt around him and the fact that he wanted to wait before they had sex made him that much more attractive to her. It gave them room to connect on higher levels and deeper depths.

She put the bouquet from Dennis on her desk and begin to throw the others away.

"So you're going to throw them all away?"

Karen turned to look at Marge, who had looked up from her crossword puzzle. "Yes. I want nothing that Kyle has sent here for me."

Once she discarded all the bouquets, she grabbed her phone to text Dennis.

***

The NBA season was off to a great start, and

Karen was looking forward to her promotion to broadcast her home team's games. She would sit alongside the infamous Stacey King to cover the Bulls games.

The Bulls first game wasn't until that Friday night, so she was able to sit back and enjoy watching the other games already happening around the league. She sat in the bar at her favorite sports grill. Every screen in it showcased a different game being played across the country. The crowd was filled with cheers and boos at the same time.

Karen arrived before Dennis. She found a booth near the back of the bar facing a screen showing the Golden State Warriors against the Brooklyn Nets. She favored the aggressive style of play of the Warriors over the relaxed motions of the Nets.

She ordered a drink and began to pay grave detail to the game, thinking of how much more detailed she would have to be in her comments on the players moves during the games. Before, she only gave synopses post game and discussed highlights during her sports segment, but her promotion would require her to practically comment second by second actions of the players throughout the entire game, and since she would partner with Stacey King, she had to make sure that she could match his basketball wit. She believed she could.

In true journalist style, Karen was making notes on the Memo app on her phone when Dennis approached the table. She stood up and smiled, giving him a brief hug before she returned to her side of the booth.

He tried to hold on to her as long as he could, but he sensed her desire to end their embrace, and he let go of her. "How are you?" Dennis sat down.

"I'm good, just trying to take some notes on the game."

He paused for a second. "Your mouth is saying that you're good, but your eyes are saying otherwise."

Karen hated that her eyes gave her away every time. She mustered up a laugh. "Nothing that time won't heal." She closed the Memo app and put her phone away.

"You know you can talk to me, right?"

"Yeah."

"We've known each other for all of these years and I believe that we've become good friends. We should be able to lean on each other in times of need." He reached his hand across the table to caress Karen's.

The waitress came, interrupting him. She took their order.

Karen was oblivious to his touch. She knew Dennis was in front of her, but her mind replayed moments in time with Kyle.

"Karen, Karen?"

"Hunh?" Karen ignored the vibrations of her cell phone. She figured it could only be text messages and voicemails from Kyle as he had been the only one blowing up her phone lately.

"You didn't hear me? Oh, never mind."

Karen just smiled absentmindedly at Dennis.

"You okay?"

"Yeah, I'm fine. I just got lost in thought for a second." Karen refocused her attention on Dennis.

"A penny for your thoughts?"

"You'd need a million dollars for them." Karen threw her hands up in surrender.

Dennis smiled enjoying Karen's witty banter.

She shook her head, hoping to shake her thoughts of Kyle. "Okay, I'm in the present now. Thank you for sending me the flowers."

"You're welcome."

"That was so sweet of you."

"Sending you the flowers was no trouble at all. I would shower you with gifts and my attention all the time if you would let me…"

"So how have you been?" Karen changed the subject.

"I've been good. Just thinking about you." Dennis winked. "Congratulations on the promotion."

Karen glossed over Dennis's flirting. "Thanks. I think I'm going to enjoy covering the Bulls games. They have always been my favorite team, especially through the two three-peats and now to be a commentator for them is such an honor and an accomplishment." Karen shared an empty smile.

"So, Kyle Irving seemed to occupy your time while we were in St. Lucia. Did you hang out with him after we returned home?" Dennis already knew the answer. He had been keeping tabs on Karen, unbeknownst to her.

Why did he have to bring up Kyle? Karen's heart sank even more. "Yeah, we've pretty much spent every day together since we got back."

Dennis' jaws tightened, his eyebrows furrowed. "So are you all a couple now?"

"No."

Dennis smiled. "Working on being a couple."

"No."

Dennis wanted to do his happy dance.

"You okay? You sound so sad." Dennis reached for Karen's hand. She idly placed her hand into his. He slowly rubbed the back of it with his thumb.

The waitress placed each of their orders in front of them. They dug in.

"Do you still plan on spending every day with Kyle, or can you make room in your schedule for me?"

Karen gave Dennis a closed-mouth smile. "Yes, we can and should hang out more, but you know I'll be traveling more now that I have to cover all of the Bulls games with the network. So please don't feel like I'm putting you on the backburner."

"As long as you commit to spending time with me when you're home, then I won't feel that way." Dennis smiled and continued to catch up with Karen. He would have to make some major adjustments to his plan and fast if he really wanted it to work.

14

"Can you believe all of this that is happening with Karen and Kyle?" Melanie asked Andrew.

"Yes." Andrew shook his head. "You gotta remember, I've been with him all of his professional career. I've seen women come and go, but I gotta be honest with you, he really does care about Karen. She's different from all the other women he's dated before. He's different with her."

"How so?" Melanie's eyebrows furrowed as she spoke.

"He can tell she doesn't care for him just because of who he is or how much money he has. When a man knows that about a woman, it comforts him and lets him know that she really wants him for him. It makes him appreciate her all the more."

"So why wasn't he upfront with her about these women?" Melanie sat up straight on Andrew's chocolate suede couch. Its color blended well with the rest of the warm earthy tones he had throughout his condo.

"He hasn't dealt with these women in a long time, so they were irrelevant to him when he first got with Karen."

"Mmm hmmm." Melanie pursed her lips and narrowed her eyes at Andrew, hoping it would convince him to be honest with her.

"I'm serious. He and Mercedes were over long ago. He left her knowing that she was still messing around with her ex and had someone to keep her attention. Bear in mind, she never told him about the little girl. Trust me, I would've known about the situation and would have demanded that he take a paternity test to resolve the issue immediately. Although he and I have had our fathers around, we've seen firsthand the effects of not having a father can have on kids."

"How so?"

"Not to mention what we see in the media every day, but just a lot of the guys we knew growing up went in different directions because of not having a good man, a father, around to show them the right way. Many of them are either dead or in jail. Then there are those that have criminal records that keep them from getting good jobs to provide for themselves, let alone their families."

Melanie watched Andrew's gaze seem to shift to another place and time. She let him linger there before she spoke again.

"I guess I can understand then." Melanie wondered how she would relay this new information to Karen. She had come to feel like Kyle was the one for Karen.

Andrew pulled Melanie closer to him. She cooed.

"I just wish we didn't always have to talk about Kyle and Karen so much. I want to focus more on us. I really care about you, Melanie."

"You do?" She looked up at him with those captivating and familiar eyes of hers.

"Yes, I just don't know how to explain this feeling, this connection that's between us. It seems so unreal that we've only known each other for a short time, but I just can't shake how close I feel to you. So where do you see yourself soon? Are we headed somewhere?"

"I know that within the next five years I want to be married with kids. The art gallery will continue to do as it is so I can stay at home as much as I like and take care of the kids and just be a great wife to my husband." Melanie bit the corner of her lip looking pensively at Andrew. "Do you see a future for us?"

"I don't need to wait five years to see us spending the rest of our lives together. If I feel the way I do about you now, then in five years, you should be giving birth to at least our third child." He winked at her.

"Stop being silly." She blushed.

"I'm serious. I want to, plan to be married to you by next year." Andrew pulled Melanie closer and nibbled on her neck.

Melanie pulled away from Andrew and stared him in the face. "By next year? So you think you know me that well that you want to marry me by next year?"

Andrew's eyes matched the same intensity as Melanie's. "Yes, I knew from the moment that I laid my eyes on you that there was something about you that drew me in. I don't know how to explain it. I can't control myself around you. You know I want to give you the business." Andrew playfully thrust his pelvis in the air.

"Focus." Melanie laughed, wagging her finger in his face.

"I'm trying to, but you're just so hot." He winked at her. "Okay, back to being serious. There's just so much more I feel, like we connect on a spiritual level. Mentally. Emotionally. I just want to be with you, and I don't think that we should have to follow someone else's timeline as to how long we need to be together before we make that kind of commitment. Some people say that you at least need to be together for a year, and then you have to be engaged for another year before you decide to get married. Their opinions don't stop there."

Melanie smiled. "Okay. Continue."

"I will." Andrew laughed. "Then they say we would need to wait two years into the marriage before we decide to have kids to make sure that we really want to stay married. That timeline sucks to me. My plan is better. I know that I want to spend the rest of my life with you, and I know that now."

Melanie got up from the couch and walked to Andrew's picture window. She stared at the part of the skyline she could see before it touched Lake Michigan.

He jumped up from the couch to stand next to her at the window. "What's wrong? Should I not have been honest with you?"

"It's not that there is something wrong. To be honest, I feel the way that you do, but this is still so new to me. I feel like we should take some more time and really get to know each other before we declare our 'love' for one another, let alone talk about making a commitment to one another like marriage." Melanie turned towards him. "I feel, I know, I have deep feelings for you, but I can't say that I love you so soon. I have to know for certain, without a shadow of a doubt that I'm in love with you before I would even agree to marry you. I'm not even ready to call you my boyfriend just yet." Melanie cast her eyes down.

Andrew's eyes widened. "So we're not official yet?"

Melanie looked at him incredulously. "No. I think we're in that courting-dating space, where we're getting to know each other. You know some people say it takes three months for a person to show their true colors." Melanie smirked.

"I just told you I don't care what other people say. I feel like when people know that they are meant to be together they should be because they know the connection they have between them is real."

"I get that, but I can't help the idea of wanting to play it safe rather than feeling bad about my choices later on down the road. I think that if we just allow time to go on, our connection will only get stronger.

Let's just let more time evolve before we say I love you or talk about marriage again."

Andrew sighed. "I know how I feel, but I respect the fact that you're not ready for such a serious conversation just yet. We will just continue to have fun and spend as much time together as we have been." Andrew pulled her closer to him. "You know, another part of getting to know someone is meeting and getting to know their family."

Melanie tensed up in his arms.

"My family is not too far from our places, so you could meet them anytime you want to." His eyes lit up. "Your family is here, too. I really want to meet your mom. So when can I meet her?"

Melanie's eyes shifted back and forth, her hands sweating. "Now is not the time to meet my mother." She bit her nails.

"Not now, like right now, silly. In the upcoming weeks?"

She rubbed his arms trying to calm her nerves and reassure him. "Time will definitely tell us when it's time to meet each other's folks. I just think that we should get to know each other a little more and be around each other more before we go as far as meeting family."

"Are you embarrassed of me?"

Melanie openly stared at him. "How could I ever be embarrassed of you? I mean, you have it all together. You're handsome, you're smart, and you're strong." She squeezed his triceps. "You're living your dreams through your job. You have this wonderful place." She spread her arms high and wide spinning around in the living room. "You have so much to offer a girl, so I'm definitely not embarrassed of you. It's just not time to meet the folks yet." Melanie's eyes shifted back towards the window.

Andrew sighed. "Clearly, we have different viewpoints on dating and how quickly things should move, but I hope that you'll see how important it is to me to meet your mom and dad, and for you to meet my parents ASAP. Family is important to me."

Melanie saw sadness in his eyes. "Don't worry, you'll meet them soon enough."

"I mean honestly, I'm eager to meet the woman that gave you life." He pecked at her lips. "That helped to mold the beautiful woman that stands in front of me." He pulled her closer to him. "So there's no chance I can meet her any sooner than your 'three-month' rule?"

The faint sound of Marvin Gaye's song, "What's Going On?", was heard coming from Melanie's purse. She knew exactly who it was from the ringtone. "I have to go now."

Andrew's eyebrows furrowed.

"I'll call you when I get home. Good night." She rushed out the door.

15

Melanie walked through the doors of the shoe store in the Old Town neighborhood talking as if Karen was right behind her.

"I'm right, aren't I?" Melanie gave a store employee a curt nod.

There was silence.

"Karen, did you hear me?" Melanie turned to see why Karen had not responded to her and saw that she had retreated back down the street.

She walked over to Karen, who was shuddering. "Karen, I know it's a little windy out here today, but you're dang near shaking like it's below zero freezing temps." Melanie pulled her arm, but she wouldn't budge.

"Karen, come on. Let's get in the store since you're so cold."

"I'm not cold." Karen pulled away from Melanie.

"Well why won't you come in the store then? It was your idea to come here in the first place."

"I know, but..."

"But what?" Melanie threw her hands up in confusion.

"I thought I saw Kyle in there."

"Kyle?"

Melanie backed up down the sidewalk until she stood directly in front of the floor to ceiling window of the store that showcased the latest running gear and shoes. She stood there peering through the window looking like a step above a window shopper but a step below a stalker. She lacked that deranged stare most of them had for the object of their attraction to be considered such.

She teetered on her toes trying to get the best possible look at the man Karen assumed to be Kyle.

He instinctively turned around and caught Melanie peering at him through the window. His eyebrows raised in bewilderment, but he waved at her, then continued his conversation with the shoe salesman.

Melanie shook her head and laughed as she walked back over to Karen who now seemed to be sweating. "Um, I see how you could confuse that man with Kyle. He's tall and bald-headed with dark caramel colored skin, but his unibrow and seemingly crooked teeth distinguish him from not being Kyle." Melanie laughed again.

"What?" Karen scrunched her face.

The door to the shoe store opened and out walked the man Karen feared was Kyle. He walked over to Melanie. "Hello, where you trying to get my attention?"

Melanie had to gather her wits before she could speak to him. Her eyes were fixated on his crooked, yellow teeth as her nostrils were being accosted by his rancid breath. His closeness to her had her senses in disarray.

Karen stifled her laughter knowing why Melanie couldn't speak for herself. "Sorry, sir. We mistook you for someone else."

"Oh, I wish I were him that you wanted, pretty lady." He leaned in closer to Melanie.

She gripped her stomach.

"I'm sorry, sir. I need to get my friend inside to get some water." Karen grabbed Melanie's arm.

"Okay." He looked defeated. "Enjoy the rest of your day." He perked up again, smiled and winked at Melanie before walking off.

Melanie staggered into the shoe store followed by Karen buckling over with laughter. They managed to make it to the first bench they saw to sit down and recompose themselves.

"One minute I found myself trying to get you out of disarray and the next minute you had to cover for me."

Karen laughed. "I know, right? I could smell the foulness of his breath from where I was, so I knew you had to be near death with how he was all up in your face."

"Girl, I was looking at death in the face and smelling it all at the same time. Jeesh. How could a man seem so attractive far away and yet when you're close to him, all hope is lost?" Melanie put her head down to control her laughter.

Karen gripped her stomach, tired of laughing.

"Hello, can I help you ladies?" the perky, young saleswoman asked.

"We just came to look at some new running shoes." Karen said, grinning.

"Well, we have—"

"I'm sorry to cut you off, but if you could give us a second alone, we'll call you back over in a bit. Thanks," Karen said.

"Okay. Well just let me know when you're ready." She walked back to the sales counter.

"Are my eyebrows still on?" Melanie asked, patting at her face.

"What?" Karen's eyebrows furrowed. "What is wrong with you?"

"I'm traumatized. His breath was so hot, I think he burned my eyebrows off." Melanie continued to rub at her eyebrows, making sure they were still there.

"You are silly," Karen said.

"No, this is all your fault."

"What? How so?" Karen shook her head slightly in confusion.

"If you wouldn't be so obsessed with Kyle then you wouldn't have been paranoid about that man being Kyle thus making me appear to ogle at the man thus making him approach me."

"Thus you sound crazy," Karen said, snapping her neck.

Melanie clamped her lips tight to suppress her laughter before she spoke. "I'm not crazy. You were afraid that was Kyle and wanted to avoid him because you still want him."

"Yeah, whatever. Change of subject. What's the latest on you and Andrew?"

"Our time together is great when we don't spend so much of it talking about you and Kyle."

Karen laughed. "I don't know why. There is no me and Kyle."

"Because he and Kyle are best friends, so Kyle's always trying to get him to put in a good word to me to put in with you." Melanie gave Karen a hard smile feigning her annoyance with Andrew always bringing the two of them up. She stood up and headed to a wall display of shoes. "Besides, Andrew likes you for Kyle, so he doesn't mind scheming to get you two together. Are you ever going to give Kyle another chance?"

"Nope." Karen joined Melanie at the shoe display picked up a pair of running shoes, but put them back down remembering that she already had the pair.

"So you've completely rid yourself of that kismet connection that you had with him?"

"Completely." Karen dropped the Asics shoe she was holding.

"Stop lying. If you were really over him, the mere mention of his name wouldn't unnerve you so much."

"Whatever. I'm as cool as a fan." Karen finally managed to put the shoe back, walked around Melanie, and grabbed a colorful New Balance gym shoe.

"Another tell-tale of yours. Your comebacks are so lame and cliché-ish when you're lying."

Karen held her hand up as if to say "no more."

Melanie ignored Karen's dramatic hand gesture and said, "Like you said before, you still have feelings for him. So why don't you give it a chance?"

"I've told you several times before, I won't be played by anyone, not anymore. Athletes think that because they can get any woman they want, they can treat a woman any kind of way. Nope. Not me."

"Have you ever just dealt with safe? You shine in a male dominated industry, but you choose to play it safe when it comes to love? Mmph."

"Yes, I'll continue to play it safe."

Melanie took the shoe from Karen's hand and made her face her

"Look, I know it's hard when it comes to your heart, but you don't want to share it with just anyone. I don't think you'd be playing it safe if you got involved with Dennis."

"Melanie, you know I love you to pieces, but for heaven's sake, would you stop nagging me about this?"

"Nope."

"It's settled already. Kyle won't have any of my time, and it's not like I'm settling for Dennis. He came on to me before Kyle did. So maybe it's Dennis I'm supposed to be with, even though we aren't serious or anything. I'm just spending time with him, getting to know him."

"Ugh." Melanie crossed her arms in contest.

"Whatever. Dennis is a great guy, if I decide to go there with him. He's at the top of his game job-wise. He's just as much into sports as I am, and we have other things in common."

Melanie pursed her lips. "Like what?"

"We're both the only child of our parents."

"You and I have that in common too, but that doesn't mean that you and I should be a couple."

Karen tried not to laugh, but she couldn't contain her laughter, and soon Melanie joined in with her.

"Stop it, silly. Anyway, he's cool to hang out with." Karen was intent on keeping a positive outlook of Dennis. "Enough about me, what about you and Andrew?"

"Like I said, since day one, we just clicked. We make sense together. It's just unexplainable." Melanie smiled, holding herself, thinking about the way Andrew always held her. She squeezed the shoe she was holding.

"What? You're looking as if you know how he feels. I mean, like how he really feels." Karen raised a lone curious eyebrow.

Melanie narrowed her eyes at Karen. "Now wait a minute."

"I'm just saying. You have that glow on your face as if you've tasted the fruit and it was good." Karen's lips pressed flat awaiting Melanie's response.

The perky saleswoman walked past and could sense they were still heavily involved in their conversation. She walked off to assist a couple nearby.

Although the store wasn't too crowded, Melanie still leaned into Karen and whispered, "We haven't gotten that far yet, and you know I wouldn't so soon. Every time we kiss there seems to be some random interruption preventing us from going any further."

"Maybe it's just God making a way of escape for you."

"Yeah, calming the temptation before I fall into it. However, I wouldn't mind..."

"Ooh, you nasty." Karen jokingly shook her head at Melanie.

"Whatever. Andrew is just right for me. Fine, tall, smooth chocolate skin, and a body like he's the pro athlete. I know that he works out every day." Melanie slowly licked her lips. "He can work me out any time."

"Ewww. TMI. Stop drooling and get it together, young lady." Karen laughed.

"You're right. Okay, I'm back to being a lady. So, you haven't even spoken to Kyle?"

"Really? You go back to talking about him? You can hush with that." Karen waved dismissively at Melanie. "I need to get home and get ready to go out with Dennis. No need to bring up Kyle. Matter of fact, that name is banned from our friendship." Karen put the shoe back she was holding and headed toward the door.

Melanie blinked rapidly. "Are you serious?"

"Yes, I'm absolutely serious." Karen worked hard to contain her laughter. "I will no longer be your friend if you mention his name again."

"You're being ridiculous." Melanie caught up to Karen. "You cover all the Bulls games for god's sake. You know you're bound to have several run-ins with him. Especially when he's the dominant player in the game. You might have to interview him up close and on camera at the end of the broadcast."

"Well, if I absolutely have to do that, then I'll be professional about it when the time comes. But I don't want any personal talk about Kyle, what's his last name?"

"You know exactly what his last name is." Melanie lifted a single eyebrow at Karen.

Karen ignored Melanie's comment as they headed to her car.

"So where are you and Dennis going?" Melanie asked as she closed the passenger door and buckled her seatbelt.

"Dennis is my date for a sports gala." Karen started her car. She felt her phone vibrating in her purse and rummaged through to find it. Her voicemail alert signaled that a message was left. "Ugh. That's Kyle again. I swear I'm going to have to get my number changed. He calls and texts me nonstop." She looked into her rearview mirror and swept her bang to the side.

"Stop being so dramatic. He calls and texts you because he wants you just like you want him."

"A lie." Karen looked in her side mirror and shifted gears before pulling into traffic.

Karen's text message alert sounded again. Melanie grabbed the phone from the middle console of the car.

She read the text aloud. "Karen, I won't stop reaching out to you. You know how special you are to me. Please give me another chance to explain the situation. I need to see you and talk to you. I miss you."

Karen shook her head. "Yeah, I need to change my number first thing in the morning."

16

Dennis had memorized Karen's schedule down to a T. He wanted to make as many plans with her to occupy all of her free time rather than letting Kyle possibly worm his way back into her life.

He wanted to pick her up for their date that night, but his work schedule made it difficult to do so. He was glad she was willing to meet him at the restaurant instead of refusing the offer since he wouldn't be able to pick her up.

Dennis: Just making sure that we're still on for tonight?

Karen: Of course. I'll meet you at the sports bar at 8.

Dennis: No, I'm thinking of somewhere else, something a little bit more cozy.

Karen: Well, where do you have in mind?

Dennis: Gibson's Steakhouse.

Karen: Okay, I've never been there before, but sounds good. See ya then.

His plan was flowing smoothly.

***

Melanie let herself into Karen's condo again. She found her in the bathroom grooming herself, as usual. She ran to her.

"Oh my god. I've missed you so much." Melanie almost squeezed Karen's ribs together as she continued to hug her.

"I've missed you, too, but I also miss my breathing. Back up off me."

Melanie shrugged halfheartedly at Karen. "So where are you off to tonight?" Melanie asked.

"Dennis asked me to meet him at Gibson's Steakhouse."

"So, is it a date?"

"Nope, I don't think so."

"Not that I'm mad about it, but why is it not a date tonight and you've been spending all your free time with him?" Melanie cocked her head to the side.

"Don't be jealous, pumpkin. I'll always love you." Karen tried to squeeze Melanie's cheeks, but Melanie moved before Karen could.

"I say it's not a date because he's not picking me up. I'm meeting him there." Karen played with her bang, moving it from one side of her face to the other.

"What does that have to do with anything?"

"I, along with countless other women, only consider an encounter with a man to be a date when he picks me up in his car and drops me off at home, making sure that I'm safe. An 'I'm home' text at the end of the night from me to him is not what I consider romantic, let alone date-like."

"You can be so modern and traditional all at the same time." Melanie shook her head, smiling at Karen.

"Whatever. I thought we would stick to going to sports bars since that's in our line of work, but I guess he wants something a little different tonight."

"So what's going on with you and Kyle?"

"Absolutely nothing," Karen screamed. "As I told you last time."

Melanie frowned. "So how's work going?"

"I'm definitely enjoying covering the games. Stacey King is hilarious and he keeps me on my toes. I'm studying the players moves more and the coaches plays to be able to say the best thing to entertain the audience and give the most thorough and accurate report of each game."

"What do you do when you see Kyle? I mean you're pretty much traveling with the team."

"I avoid him at all costs." Karen smirked.

"You know you only avoid him because you still have feelings for him. Otherwise, you would face him head on."

"Whatever. I'm not into him." Karen smirked. "I just want to avoid him because he's annoying. Since I changed my number, and he no longer has it, he's resorted to writing subliminal messages on his Facebook, Instagram, and Twitter accounts. Even when they're doing their warm-ups before the games and I'm on the sideline prepping, he still manages to try and get my attention and talk to me while he should be practicing his shots." Karen decided on keeping her bangs on the left side of her face.

"What do you mean about the subliminal messages?" Melanie's eyebrows raised as she grabbed Karen's eye shadow palette eyeing the vast array of colors.

"Look at this." Karen opened the Facebook app on her phone and went to Kyle's page. She showed Melanie how for one week straight, Kyle posted the lyrics to songs that he and she both loved and listened to almost nonstop during the time they were together.

TheRealKyleIrving
Tuesday at 12:33 a.m.
When I feel what I feel
Sometimes it's hard to tell you so
You may not be in the mood to learn what you
think you know

TheRealKyleIrving
Wednesday at 11:20 p.m.
There are times when I find
You want to keep yourself from me
When I don't have the strength; I'm just a mirror
of what I see

TheRealKyleIrving
Thursday at 3:30 a.m.
But at your best you are love
You're a positive motivating force within my life
Should you ever feel the need to wonder why

Let me know, let me know. . .

TheRealKyleIrving
Friday at 2:05 a.m.
When you feel what you feel
Oh, how hard for me to understand
So many things have taken place before this love
affair began

TheRealKyleIrving
Saturday at 2:33 a.m.
But if you feel, oh, like I feel
Confusion can give way to doubt
For there are times when I fall short of what I
say, what I say I'm all about, all about...

TheRealKyleIrving
Sunday at 2:33 a.m.
But at your best you are love
You're a positive motivating force within my life
Should you ever feel the need to wonder why
Let me know, let me know. . .

Karen finished scrolling through Kyle's posts. "See, by Sunday night, he put up all of the lyrics to our favorite song."

Melanie finally put the makeup palette back where she got it from. "You're so full of yourself. How do you know those posts were about you?" Melanie laughed hard.

"Whatever. I know because we played that song every time before we left each other's presence. He would send me lines of it in text messages daily, and I would respond with the next line of the song. That's how I know he posted that song and the others for me. Thank you very much," Karen said, raising her voice as she reached for a tube of mascara.

Melanie watched Karen furtively. "Okay, you're making it seem as if he's trying to interact with you all the time. That's just Facebook."

"Instagram too." Karen opened her Instagram account to show Melanie his page and the different songs he posted there every day over the past couple of weeks. "We would always play music in the background when we were together. We had a playlist of the songs we loved. They reminded us of each other. He's posted the lines of so many of those songs between his different social media accounts. He's even put some of the lyrics from the songs as the quote of the day on his own website."

"Maybe they are for you." Melanie put a piece of gum in her mouth. "Why the sudden frown?"

"I guess I just got sad all of a sudden thinking on how close he and I had become. He knew I grew up largely on old school R&B, so whenever we listened to it, we cuddled, and he held me tightly knowing that those moments with him reminded me of my parents." Karen sniffled, not ready to cry or continue being so melancholy. "Anywho, I know he's been talking to me and about me through social media and even the media."

"Okay. So what other evidence do you have to support your theory?" Melanie laughed and displayed a bright smile, trying to further lighten up the mood in the bathroom.

Karen lifted a single eyebrow at Melanie before laughing. "Well, I saw that he did an interview last week with *People* and they asked him if he had a love interest."

Melanie perked up.

"He said yes."

"I wonder who she is." Melanie smirked.

"Will you just let me finish the story?" Karen turned her back from the mirror to rest her butt on the countertop. She looked at Melanie relaxing on the big ottoman in the middle of the bathroom. "The interviewer asked him when the public would get a chance to meet this lucky woman. He said as soon as she accepts that she is the love of his life."

Melanie threw up her hands and her mouth slackened. "That's all that he said?"

"Uh, yes. The interviewer tried to get more information about 'the love of his life', but he refused to share more."

Melanie shook her head. "And you still think he was talking about you?"

"Yes." Karen smiled unknowingly. "He did three other interviews and he gave more and more details about me, 'the love of his life', and in one he even mentioned that the woman was a runner he met on a running trail one morning. He said that she, me, actually bumped into him and fell head over heels for him."

"Girl no he didn't." Melanie cupped her mouth trying to stifle her laughter.

"Yes, he did, but he laughed and cleared it up with the interviewer that he was just kidding, that she didn't fall in love with him at that time, she just literally almost fell. I think he cleared it up knowing that I would be really upset with him if he didn't." Karen pursed her lips.

Melanie shook her head. "Maybe he is talking about you."

"I know he is. You know how the end of every game the sportscaster interviews the player on the winning team who had the best night?" Karen didn't even wait for Melanie to answer her, she just kept talking. "Well, Kyle was that player last night." Karen tried to suppress her smile. "Instead of him answering the questions asked and recapping the game, he stood there and said, 'Will you please forgive me and give me another chance?'"

Melanie's mouth gaped open. "Are you serious?"

"Yes. The sportscaster was so confused. He asked Kyle more questions about the game. If he was enjoying living back in his hometown, but the only responses he gave were 'I'm sorry.' Of course the sportscaster seemed thrown off. He looked like he wanted to ask Kyle who was he talking to and why was he sorry, but the guy remained professional and asked Kyle one last question. He asked Kyle how was he able to get so many offensive rebounds. Do you know he ignored the sportscaster's question but responded saying, 'Will you please forgive me and give me another chance?' He ended the interview and walked past me with pleading eyes as he headed to the locker room."

"Wow. He really does have a jones in his bones for you."

"I don't care if he has a jones in his bones or stars in his eyes for me. We're not going to happen."

"So you still haven't talked to him about those women?"

"No. Really, Melanie, I haven't talked to him and I'm not going to." Karen turned back to the mirror trying to decide what else she should do to spruce herself up.

"Well, when I talked to Andrew, he said he knows for a fact that Kyle didn't know about Mercedes being pregnant because if Kyle did, they would have made sure that they got a paternity test from day one to determine if Kyle was the father."

"I don't care if you want to believe what your man says, I don't have to..."

Melanie cleared her throat. "Whatever. He's not my man."

"Kyle and I stopped talking, but you two have continued to 'talk'. So what do you call him if he's not your man?"

"I call him my friend." Melanie's eyes danced, and her lips curved into a smile.

"Whatever." Karen cocked her head at Melanie.

"Yeah, we spend a lot of time together when he's not catering to Kyle or busy with the new clients he's picked up in the D-League for the NBA."

"He has other clients? So what does that mean for Kyle?" Karen asked, concerned.

"Kyle is definitely still his number one client. And remember they are best friends, like brothers, so I don't think anything will break up that duo."

"Good. Well, can you please tell Andrew to tell Kyle to leave me alone? Because I don't want to have anything to do with him. I don't care if he didn't know about Mercedes and her baby. There's still those other two chicks out there that constantly post about their relationships with Kyle."

"Technically, they weren't in relationships with him," Melanie retorted.

"I don't care what kind of 'ship' you want to call it. They had interactions and babies were the products. I won't deal with it." Karen turned to face Melanie. "Why should I have to be a stepmother before I even become a mother?" Karen frowned.

Melanie shrugged her shoulders.

"Don't get me wrong, I'm not saying that I'm going to ostracize men who have kids and say that I'll never date them, because I know life happens. However, I want to enjoy my husband and not have to deal with him and his three baby mommas. There might be more out there. Besides two of them are still pregnant, so there's no telling what type of living hell they would try to put me through being pregnant with his kids, not to mention after they have the kids. All of that baby momma drama is not the vision that I have for my life. I want to live a peaceful-fun-filled life. I don't want to deal with that crap."

"You sure have a mouthful to say whenever the topic is Kyle." Melanie smirked. "And who's to say those are his kids?"

"The two pregnant hoodrats."

"Well, since you think they're 'hoodrats', do they seem like the types that you should believe?"

"At this point, I'll believe them before I believe Kyle. I can't tell you enough how I asked him if there was anything from his past that would threaten us and he told me over and over again there wasn't. I'm just not ready for any drama in my life right now. Anyway, I need to finish getting ready to hang out with Dennis."

"You mean go out on your date with Dennis, right?" Melanie laughed.

"No, I know what I'm saying. We're just hanging out."

"Did he pay for everything the last time you all 'hung out'?"

"Yes."

"Did he make sure you got home safely?"

"Yes."

"How often do you talk to him?"

"Pretty much every day and often throughout the day."

"Well, that doesn't just sound like 'hanging out' to me."

"It is right now."

"Whatever. And besides, you never get this dolled up when we just 'hang out'." Melanie laughed and pulled Karen's hair.

"Well, I say I'm not, and I have the final say so." Karen laughed. "I'll talk to you later. I need to hurry up and get ready for my 'non-date' with Dennis. I have to make my way over to Gibson's Steakhouse." Karen licked her lips. "I've never been there before, but I heard they have a really good turtle ice cream cake for dessert. I'm hungry."

"You and your ice cream. I'm pretty sure you'll be running when you get back."

"You know it." Karen winked. "I'll talk to you later."

"Okay. Let me know when you make it in tonight, girl."

***

Karen walked into Gibson's Steakhouse and noticed just how quaint and cozy the atmosphere was. She laughed out loud thinking about how Melanie kept calling it a date. The more she looked around at all the couples cooing at each other, she realized maybe Dennis did think it was a date.

"Hello. Welcome to Gibson's Steakhouse. Would you like to sit at the bar, a table, or a booth?" The maitre'd greeted Karen.

"Hello. Dennis Michaels should have a table reserved for us already."

The maitre'd checked her list. "Yes, he's already here. Hope here will escort you to your table. Enjoy your dinner."

Dennis saw Karen. He stood and scanned her from head to toe as she walked towards him. *God she is fine!* He loved the way her dress hugged her curves and the ankle boots she wore elongated her sexy legs. He tried to keep his face from showing his thoughts.

Karen smiled as she approached him. "Hi. How are you?"

Dennis reached for her and gave her a firm hug, cradling her at the small of her back.

She admitted to herself that there was something different in the hug he gave her. It wasn't a greeting they had shared before.

"You look beautiful tonight, as always." He allowed her to scoot into her side of the booth before he sat on his side.

"And you look dapper, as always."

"Dapper?" He laughed.

"Yes."

"Well thank you."

Karen laughed to herself.

"What's funny?"

"Oh, nothing." She found herself laughing even harder.

"Come on, what's so funny, I want to laugh, too."

"It's nothing."

Dennis's furrowed eyebrows let Karen know he really wanted in on what she thought was so funny.

"It's just that Melanie was over my house before I left. She knew that I was going out with you again, so she asked where we were going on a date. A 'date' as if we're dating." Karen laughed, but she stopped when she noticed the solemn look on Dennis's face. "What?"

"It's not that funny to me because I like you, and I feel like we are dating."

Karen sat up straight. She cleared her throat. "Dating? Us dating?"

"Yes. I mean I know we've never talked about it, but I was going to bring it up sooner than later. I just feel like we have such a great time with one another. I don't want moments like these to ever end." He sat up straighter. He fiddled with the silverware near him. "I really like you and I have to be honest, Karen, I've liked you since the day I met you."

Karen was silent.

"My intention of meeting you in St. Lucia was to get to know you more and to share how I really felt about you, but Kyle got in the way."

Karen was so unnerved by the mention of Kyle's name that she overlooked Dennis's admission that he intentionally went to St. Lucia knowing she was there.

"What? Did I say something wrong?" Dennis wasn't sure if she heard his slip of the tongue. His palms clammed up.

"No, it's nothing. Back to what you were saying about us dating and liking me." Karen smiled.

"I have to be honest. I was feeling you way before Kyle came along. So, are you interested in me? Would you be willing to give us a chance?"

"I could tell there was something between you and me in St. Lucia, and I was kind of giving the thought of us room in my head before I talked to him." Karen sighed. "You and I have been friends for so long, but that was mainly at work. I didn't want to start something romantic with you. It not work out, and then we have bad vibes with one another and it show up where we work. I didn't want to take that risk and pursue it." She lowered her eyes.

"Truth moment?"

"Of course." Karen smiled.

"Do you still have feelings for Kyle?" Dennis asked pensively.

"Uh, uh, uh, no. Why would you ask that?" Karen gulped down some of her water.

"Seems like every time I bring his name up your mood changes." He paused waiting for her to speak.

She said nothing but gave him a half-hearted smile.

"I mean, I really do want to be with you. I know that my feelings for you are strong and although I know you're definitely worth the chase, I don't want to have to compete for your heart if he's still in it." Dennis stared intensely at her.

"No, it's not that. I'm definitely over him. It's not like he and I were even a couple. I'm definitely over him." Karen scratched her ear.

Dennis perked up. "So you and I are together now?"

"Together? Us? You and I?" Karen's eyes shifted back and forth before she decided to speak again. "Wow. That would be a big leap from where we are now. How about we say that we're dating. Like just-going-on-dates-to-get-to-know-each-other-better kind of dating? And we can see where that takes us."

Dennis nodded. He would do things her way, for now.

"Okay. I'll just give you a heads up. Even though we're just dating, I'm not going to date anyone else. Karen, I just want to be with you. I'm not saying that you can't date anyone else, but that would be nice." Dennis said the last part under his breath. "I'm not interested in being with another woman. I just want to spend as much time as possible getting to know you."

"Oh really?" Karen's eyebrows raised.

"Yeah, really." Dennis gave her an easy nod. "You're already out of town a lot with your job. I definitely want to give you my undivided attention when you're here. I wanna show you that I care about you when you're gone, too."

Karen smiled, but not the way Kyle could make her smile.

17

Karen was in her dressing room when there was a knock at the door. "Come in."

"Hey. How are you?" Dennis stood in the doorway.

"Hey. Good, but what are you doing here?" Karen asked.

"Well, I guess you didn't get the memo. Stacey King is sick and can't cover tonight's game with you. Guess who they asked?" Dennis stood there with big eyes, smiling, and his arms outstretched wide.

"Wait, they asked you?" Karen's eyebrows furrowed.

"Yes. You said that as if I'm not worthy of covering the game with you." Dennis playfully poked his lips out.

"No, it's nothing like that." Karen stood up and walked towards Dennis, "It's just that I thought they might have had Brett Donner, but hey, who better to share my night with than you." She winked at him.

"That's what I was thinking." Dennis smiled.

They hugged each other. Dennis attempted to kiss Karen, but she averted his lips. He still held her tightly.

She admitted to herself that she liked him, but she wasn't ready to get physical in any way with him just yet, even though they had been dating for a few months.

"Karen, I know this is not the time or place for this discussion, but are you afraid to kiss me or something?"

"No, why would you say that?"

"These last few times we've gone out, I try to end the night with a harmless kiss, but you always seem to turn your head and I end up kissing your jaw." Dennis pouted. "I'm sorry if I've offended you by trying to kiss you and you think I'm moving too fast, but it's just that you're so beautiful and your lips look so soft. I just want to know how they feel."

Karen was silent.

"I'm sorry if I make you uncomfortable."

"No, it's not that. It's just that I want to take my time with us. Like I said, I don't want to do anything that would cause any weird vibes between us if we didn't work out."

"Why are you so sold on us not working out?" He sighed, rubbing his face. "Am I your type or not?"

"Of course you are, Dennis. Don't get me wrong. I really like you. I'm just in a phase in my life where I want to make sure that what I'm doing is right because whatever it is, I want it to last." She walked away from him and back over to her makeup kit and toyed with the blush brush. "I don't want to call you my man today, but we're broken up by tomorrow because we realized we aren't really for each other. I don't want to play games. Whoever I commit to now is who I want to be with for the rest of my life. Do you understand what I'm saying?"

"Yeah, I get what you're saying." Her back was towards him as he walked closer to her frowning.

"Thanks." Karen smiled and turned to face him.

"Are you ready to go and have fun broadcasting this game?"

"Definitely." She looked back in the mirror one last time.

"Trust me, you look great."

She smiled.. "Thanks."

He smiled. "Let's go. We're late."

"What?" Karen's eyes widened as she looked at her watch. She looked up aiming beady eyes at Dennis. "You see why I didn't want to mix business with pleasure. Messing around with you, I'm late."

He smiled. "Oh don't worry. It'll be okay."

She snarled playfully. "You better hope so." She yanked his arm and they flew out of the dressing room headed to the court.

They walked out into the arena headed to where the other sportscasters from various networks sat on the sideline right in between the Bulls bench and the visitor's bench.

The Bulls were playing the Boston Celtics that night. Kyle and his teammates were already on the floor shooting around.

Dennis had calmed Karen's nerves by the time they made it in the arena. They walked past Kyle and knowing he had and audience, Dennis leaned in close to Karen to whisper to her, knowing what he said to her would make her giddy and giggle like a school girl getting her first Valentine's Day card from her crush. She did just that.

Kyle stared at them the entire time. His ears were hot, and he was even more pissed when he got hit in the face with the ball that he was supposed to catch instead of staring down Dennis as he flirted with Karen.

"Come on, Kyle, man. Get your head in the game," the power forward said.

"Man, the game hasn't even started," Kyle said.

"So what? Practice makes perfect. We're on a winning streak, and we don't want to break it. We can't afford any slip-ups. You've been doing a great job so far, so we definitely need your best tonight to keep us winning," the power forward said.

"I'll be ready, Gibson. Don't worry about it." Kyle turned from Gibson and made eye contact with Dennis. He stared at him long and hard.

Dennis didn't flinch.

Kyle didn't miss catching the pass this time, and he made sure his shot was nothing but net.

The team moved on to practicing lay-ups.

"What are you doing? Karen asked.

"Nothing." Dennis continued to caress the back of Karen's hand.

"We're at work. You can't be flirting with me now and carrying on the way you are." Karen's eyes were stern, but she smiled.

"Says who?"

"Says me. We're not on a date. We're at work right now, so we have to be professional and keep the flirting at bay."

"Says who?" Dennis leaned in closer to her, smiling.

Her lips flattened and she focused her sight on him. "Says me."

Dennis caressed her hand again. "But I won't get to see you again until next week. You all go on a six-game road stretch, and I won't see you until it's over."

"There's always video chatting." Karen giggled.

"But there's nothing like face to face time with you." Dennis pouted feigning sadness.

"I know it's sad that you won't get to see this face in person, but thanks to modern technology we can see, talk, and text each other as much as the day will allow until it's time for me to cover the games." Karen adjusted her headset.

"Wouldn't it be great if Stacey King was still sick and couldn't make it for the road stretch?"

"It might be great for us, it might be great for you, but I don't think it would be great for Stacey if he was sick that long."

Dennis's eyes shifted. "Yeah, you're right."

The game started, and the broadcasting chemistry flowed effortlessly between Karen and Dennis. If one wasn't an avid fan or follower of the Bulls, he or she would think that the duo always covered the games together. For the first two quarters, the banter flowed freely between them.

Half time came and brought a flurry of entertainment to center court while the players went to the locker rooms.

"Hey. Do you want something to snack on?" Dennis asked.

"Please." Karen clutched her hands in a praying motion. "I'm starving."

Dennis laughed. "Sure. And next time don't sit there hungry. Let me know. It's my duty to take care of you."

"How were you going to get me something to eat and you were on the clock as I was?" Karen laughed.

Dennis smirked. "Trust me. I have a way of getting what I want." He winked at her and walked off. He was glad to break away from her. Not only was he hungry, but he also needed to make a few phone calls to ensure that his plan was still flowing smoothly. He was still gone when the teams came back out during half time to shoot around.

Kyle managed to break away from the shooting and made his way over to Karen. "What happened to Stacey tonight?"

Karen ignored him.

"Karen, what happened to Stacey? He normally covers the games with you."

"He's sick." Karen didn't even bother to look at him.

"Oh. I hope he gets better soon. So, how have you been doing?" He held the ball under his arm.

She ignored him.

"You look great."

She freshened up her lip gloss.

"How long are you going to keep ignoring me, Karen? Can't we talk about this?" Kyle became annoyed thinking about how much he saw Karen talking to Dennis, yet she sat there in front of him refusing to utter any words. "Oh, so you can't talk to me because you're with him? That douchebag."

She smoothed her hair down and pretended to check her blazer for lint.

"Karen?" Kyle waited for her to respond to him, but the only thing he heard was the roars of the crowd as the end of the halftime buzzer sounded, signaling him to go back to his bench.

Dennis walked up to the table. Kyle eyed him, channeling every ounce of hate he had for Dennis in his body to his eyes, and then walked away.

Dennis smirked knowing Kyle wouldn't act on the fury he saw in Kyle's eyes. He sat down and texted someone.

Karen covered her mouth to prevent anyone else from hearing what she was saying. "You can't be texting while we're on the job."

"Oh, don't worry about me getting caught." Dennis laughed. "But that was my last one."

They continued to go back and forth commenting on the players of both teams as the game progressed.

It was down to the last ten seconds of the game. The Bulls had possession of the ball. All they needed to do was hold on to the ball, and they would win the game.

Kyle was dribbling the ball when he looked over to the table and noticed Dennis leaning into Karen. He could tell he was flirting with her. Karen was laughing and seemed to be enjoying the attention she was getting from Dennis.

With Kyle distraught and not paying attention, the Celtics point guard stole the ball from him and made a fast break down to their end to score a three-point field goal. Time ran out on the shot clock, and the Celtics won by one point.

Kyle was so busy looking at Dennis fawn all over Karen that he didn't even realize what happened until he looked up at the scoreboard to see that his team had lost.

It was his fault.

He looked back over at Karen. She shook her head, took her headset off, and walked away.

Dennis followed behind her with his hands around her waist. He looked back at Kyle and smirked as he walked off, drawing closer to Karen.

18

Kyle was bummed. He figured his turnover from the game with the Celtics sent the Bulls on a five-game losing streak.

As much as it pained him, he reasoned that he would have to move on from Karen, seeing as though she wouldn't give him the time of day. His obsession with her seemed to distract him from going hard for what was once his number one goal—a championship ring. He was a third of the way through the season, and he knew that he needed to focus if he really was going to get that ring.

Andrew walked into the Roberto Center where the Bulls practiced and knew exactly where to find Kyle—on the court practicing his post-game. "Kyle? Kyle? What's up, man?"

Kyle excused himself from one of the assistant coaches and went to the sideline to talk to Andrew. "What's up, man?" They shook hands and gave a brotherly embrace.

"Nothing, just came to check up on you. Your game has gotten better since you all snapped the losing streak. I'm just trying to make sure you're still in a good headspace."

"You act like I didn't talk to you just the other day."

"True." Andrew laughed. "But you know I have to make sure that you're straight. I don't care about the lost games as much as I'm concerned about you as my brother."

Kyle knew what Andrew was referring to. "If you're talking about Karen, then yeah, man, I really did care about her. I loved her, and it's hard trying to let her go." Kyle rubbed his head. His heart jumped and his stomach turned nervously, admitting that out loud to someone other than Karen.

"Word?" Andrew was shocked to hear Kyle admit it, although he already knew it. He had never seen Kyle go after a woman the way he went after Karen. He knew it must have been love from the starry eyes Kyle had whenever he looked at her or spoke of her.

"But I can't keep chasing after somebody who doesn't want to be caught."

"Are you sure about that?"

"Yeah." Kyle sighed. "I'm just going to focus on making the rest of this season the best one of my career so far."

"I heard that, bro."

"So you remember we have the meeting with Mercedes later?"

"Yeah, man. How can I forget? I can't believe that I have a child. And with a woman that's not even my wife. I know I've had the results for months, but I just haven't even brought myself to tell my parents face to face. I know they heard about it from the voicemails they leave me, but I'm not ready to talk to them yet. I'm certain that they're disappointed in me. I thought I left my past in the past, but it seems it's come to haunt me, especially where Karen is concerned."

Andrew laughed.

"What are you laughing at?"

"You just said a minute ago that you can't keep chasing her if she doesn't want to be caught, or something like that, but then the next minute, you're standing here with your lip practically touching the floor and your sad puppy dog eyes saying her name and sighing. You got it bad, man." Andrew hurried up and ran from Kyle before he hit him as he knew he would try.

"I got you. I'll hit you up after practice," Kyle said.

"Alright. See you later, man," Andrew said as he walked off the court.

***

Kyle sat across from Mercedes and her lawyer as they signed the last of the papers that would legalize Kyle's parental rights to his three-year-old daughter, Gabrielle Silva.

He sat there dazed at times still not believing that Mercedes had his daughter, and he knew nothing about her. He wished he could have been there for it all, her birth, her first steps, her first words... Granted he and Mercedes were not a couple, but he would never be a deadbeat father. He planned to be the best father he could be.

"I'm glad we were able to come to an amicable agreement concerning this matter," Kyle's lawyer said.

"Thank you," Mercedes uttered.

Kyle and Mercedes lawyers shook hands before they finished putting away their perspective documents into their briefcases.

Kyle was advised not to speak to Mercedes until after everything was finalized.

His lawyer was ready to escort him out. "Come on, Mr. Irving. Let's go."

"Thanks for all your help, Mr. Warren, but I think I'll stay behind for a second and talk to Mercedes."

"Well, good luck with everything, and I'm definitely still looking into the situation with the other ladies. I'll be sure to get back to you as soon as I have some updated info."

"Thank you so much."

Mercedes lawyer walked out with Kyle's lawyer.

"Mercedes, can I talk to you for a second?" Kyle shoved his hands into his pocket. He gently rocked back and forth from his toes to his heels.

Mercedes walked towards him with her head down.

"So how have you been?"

"I'm okay, but I admit that it's been stressful dealing with all the media trying to find out information about me, you, us, Gabby."

Kyle struggled to understand Mercedes at times through her thick Portuguese accent. He smiled at the mention of Mercedes nickname for Gabrielle.

"Gabrielle, or Gabby as you call her. How is she? How is my daughter?"

Mercedes finally looked up at him. She smiled. "She's great. She's the most beautiful, energetic, and cheerful three-year-old you could ever meet. She's brought me so much joy in the midst of all this chaos."

Kyle became flustered. "Mercedes, why didn't you ever tell me about her?"

She put her head back down again. "Kyle, I, I, didn't think that she was yours at first. But as time went on, she started looking more and more like you. I was still off and on with my ex and he was around since her birth. But one day, I guess it hit him how much she looks like you, recounting I told him that I had been with you during one of our breakups. He said he knew she was yours and couldn't be around her anymore. He admitted that he never felt like she was his. I begged him to stay, but he asked for a paternity test. I agreed to do it." Mercedes frowned.

Kyle stood with his hands crossed at his chest in front of Mercedes. His forehead creased and his eyebrows furrowed as he listened to her.

"As you know, the test came back negative and he's never seen her again since that day." Mercedes turned away from Kyle and walked over to the window overlooking Lake Michigan. "I waited for a while before I thought about telling you. Honestly, I wasn't going to tell you, but I didn't want you to miss out any longer with that angel." She smiled.

Kyle walked to the window and stood next to Mercedes. "So when can I meet her?"

Mercedes faced him. "As soon as you want to."

Kyle nodded his head. "Cool." He smiled. "Like today?"

"Well, I wouldn't suggest that you come to where I'm staying here because I'm certain that my aunt's house is swamped with the paparazzi."

"Yeah, and you bringing her to my place would just be more fuel to the rumor mill. So how about I call you later and we arrange a place to meet?"

"That sounds great."

Kyle and Mercedes walked out of the room and to the elevator. The panel indicated that the elevator was still on the 35th floor and they were on the 27th floor.

"So, tell me about her," Kyle said.

Mercedes remembered that she had a picture of Gabrielle in her purse. She pulled it out and gave it to him.

He looked at the picture and the tiny him on it and smiled. He tried hard to fight back tears of pride that puddled in his lids. She looked just like him, his younger sister, and pictures of his mother when she was younger. She really was his. He smiled.

They stepped onto the elevator.

"Can I have this?" He gripped the picture tightly in his hand.

Mercedes hesitated. It was the only physical picture she had of Gabby. "I guess. I have plenty pictures of her in my phone."

"Can you send me those, too?"

"Of course."

They exited the elevator.

"Want me to walk you to your car?"

"I'm okay."

"Mercedes, I'll walk you to your car."

"Okay."

They stepped out into the Chicago winter. They thought they would be greeted by the brutal winds from the lake downtown, but instead they were swamped by the paparazzi. Out of the midst of the cameras emerged Porsha and Unique.

"I bet he just cut her a fat check, so I know I better get me one, too. And as soon as I drop this baby," Porsha declared and high-fived Unique.

"Girl, yeah. You know he has to break us off some of that money that he's making in the NBA. Me and my baby gon' be straight," Unique said.

The cameraman made sure that the mics were directly in front of Kyle to capture his responses. Luckily, Andrew was waiting in the lobby until the meeting was over with Mercedes. He caught up with Kyle the moment that he saw all the lights flashing on the sidewalk. "Okay, ladies and gentlemen, this is enough. You can go on your way. If you continue to harass my client, I'll make sure to file charges against you. And as for you two ladies, please stay away from Kyle before we have to get restraining orders against you. Our matter with you two can't be settled until the babies are born or unless you all agree to do those tests to determine paternity before the babies are born." Andrew signaled for the valet to get Kyle's car.

"Restraining orders? That ain't necessary. And I ain't stickin' no needles in me, harmin' my unborn child." Porsha spoke up first as usual.

"Nope. Not me, either. I can't afford to have no retarded baby," Unique chimed in.

Kyle shook his head in disgust at the women. He couldn't quite remember having slept with them. He figured they must have been random one night stands he forgot about before he changed his playboy-like ways. If he did, he was ashamed of himself for sleeping with women that would even say such things out of their mouths.

He looked at Mercedes, held his phone up and shook it, hoping she would know it meant he would call her later.

The valet driver pulled up with Kyle's car. He jumped in and drove off.

Mercedes walked to her car in the parking garage across the street with the paparazzi following her and hounding her to give the details of her meeting with Kyle.

Porsha and Unique stood by rubbing their bellies and high-fiving each other.

***

"Man, I just keep thinking, I'm a daddy," Kyle said as he shook his head in disbelief.

"Yeah, man. You ugly, knucklehead! You made me an uncle."

Kyle laughed. "Whatever...hold on. Mercedes is on the other line."

"Hello... yeah, I can meet you there... Okay...At six?... Cool... Thanks... See y'all then...Wait, should I bring something?" Kyle laughed. "Okay...bye."

Kyle switched back over to his call with Andrew.

"What did she say?"

"Just the time to meet her and Gabby, as she calls my daughter." Kyle smiled.

"Gabby. So, when can I meet her?" Andrew asked.

"Soon."

"You excited about this, man?"

"Yeah. I wish I would've witnessed her birth and these past three years, but I'm glad to meet her when she is so young so she can get comfortable with being around me as opposed to meeting her when she's a moody teenager, resenting me for not being there for her. Or even worse, she not wanting to have anything to do with me at all. You know these kids nowadays are jacked up from stuff like that."

"Yeah, bro. So now are you ready to talk to your parents about her yet?"

"I told you I've been kind of avoiding them because I feel like I've let them down."

"That's nonsense, man."

"I didn't want to disappoint them like this. I have a three-year-old they've never met. I had a baby out of wedlock. They didn't raise me that way. I was raised in the church, to be a husband before becoming a father. I didn't do it that way and I think they'll be hurt by that. And man, you know how much my mom has always wanted grandchildren, so for her to find out I have a three-year-old she's missed out on... I know it will hurt her."

"No, what probably hurts her more is you not talking to her about it all this time."

"Yeah, man, I hear ya. But then there's my dad." Kyle rubbed his head back and forth.

"What about him?"

"I know he'll get on me for not providing for her before now as a man should for his family, but how could I when I didn't know about her?" Kyle threw his hands up in the air.

"Man, call them as soon as you can to tell them, then arrange a good time for them to meet her."

"Yeah, you're right. As soon as I can." Kyle's silence was eerie.

"Man, what's up?" Andrew asked, wondering if the call had dropped.

"I'm still here. I'm just thinking about all of this."

"What? Those other two chicks?"

"Naw..."

"So what is it?"

Kyle remained silent.

Andrew laughed. "Don't tell me that you're still over there sulking over Karen? Man up."

"I did man up. I admitted to you that I loved her." Kyle laughed. "I'm trying to get over her, but I still have feelings for her. I keep trying to brush it off, but every now and then I just think about what life would be like if she was by my side instead of with that bum Dennis. I see her all 'booed' up with him and it makes me so angry. I wonder if she still cares about me."

"Yeah, I know you really cared about her, but you can't worry about that now. You have a daughter that you have to focus on. You have games that you have to win so you can get this ring so we can brag and pop bottles." Andrew laughed.

"The only bottles I'll be popping are Gabrielle's. Do three-year-old's even still drink from bottles?" Kyle scratched his head.

Andrew snorted from laughing so hard. "Uh, no. Man, you have a lot of learning to do when it comes to kids."

Kyle's mind drifted to Karen. "She shouldn't be happy with him...she should only be happy with me."

Andrew knew exactly who he was talking about. "Focus, man. We're talking about your daughter, not your fetish with Karen."

"Okay, okay...So what's up with you and Melanie? You two still going strong?"

"Ah, someone I love to talk about, Melanie. Yeah, man. I can't explain the connection that we share."

"You keep talking about this 'connection'. How is it any different than what any other man or couple for that matter has experienced being 'in love'?" Kyle laughed.

"Whatever. I've been in love before, but not like this. I wasn't a dog like you."

"I wasn't a dog. Let's just say that I was a connoisseur of women."

Andrew joined Kyle in laughing.

"Dude, it goes so much more deeper than being physically attracted to her. Don't get me wrong, she's fine as ever. I mean fine, but it's more than that."

"So have you seen her naked?"

"No," Andrew replied.

"After all this time?" Kyle raised his eyebrows. "Why not?"

"I just haven't. We've been taking our time."

"That's a long time. So you telling me you haven't gotten none all of this time?"

"No. There's nothing wrong with waiting...I mean, yeah I'm ready to get in that," Andrew licked his lips unknowingly, "but I won't trip if it doesn't happen just yet. 'Cuz I know what we have is real, and she's worth the wait."

"Dude, you're talking like you're in love with her. Wait, are you?"

"I think so. I have this feeling deep in the pit of my stomach that she's the one, and her eyes, there's something about her eyes. I wish I knew exactly what's so familiar about them. It's like I've seen them before. It's crazy." Andrew stared amidst.

"Man, you've talked about those eyes so many times before. I wish you would hurry up and figure them out or remember who she reminds you of because you're starting to creep me out." Kyle laughed.

"Whatever, man. I just feel good around her. I can be real with her."

"Okay. That's a good thing. Let me ask you this, y'all not having sex right, as you say?"

"I just told you we're not."

"Well, has she at least kissed you yet?" Kyle laughed.

"Yeah, man."

"Aw, okay. Well, does she know what she's doing?"

"What is this, high school?" Andrew asked.

Kyle laughed.

"Why are you worried about whether or not we've kissed?"

"I didn't ask if y'all kissed yet. I asked you if she kissed you yet, like that Usher song, 'Good Kisser'." Kyle hummed the melody of the song.

Andrew squinted his eyes and smirked. "Yeah, she's a good kisser even though it's none of your business, weirdo."

"So she's a 'lipstick on yo' legs' good kisser?" Kyle slapped his knee, laughing hysterically after he spoke.

"What?" It registered with Andrew what Kyle was asking. "Naw, man. I didn't know you were talking about that kind of kissing at first. Everything ain't about sex."

"Man, I know it's not, but still, if you two have this connection the way you say you do, then I would think that you would have explored each other sexually in some type of way." Kyle shook his head.

"Well did you do it with Karen since you were in love with her?"

"I still am and no." Kyle sighed. "She's special to me, and I needed her to see that without sex." Kyle exhaled loudly again and slumped his shoulders.

"Why are you rushing Melanie and I to do it if you understand that some women are just worth the wait?"

Kyle remained silent.

"Yeah, got you on that one, hunh?" Andrew laughed. "I ain't gon' front. I wanna be with her like that, but every time we're almost there, something interrupts us."

"Hunh? So you telling me there's always something that interrupts y'all from gettin' it on?" Kyle rubbed his forehead.

"Yeah, it's crazy. It's something going on with her mother. And don't get me started with all this foolishness I've had to do recon on for you. You think that those two harass you, but I've ran more interference for you with them than you know. It's so crazy how they just keep popping up everywhere you are, knowing your exact schedule."

"Thanks, bro."

"No problem. That's what I'm here for. Still a mystery to me how they knew exactly where the meeting with you and Mercedes would be today." Andrew shook his head. "They know too much of your schedule. I think you may need to get a restraining order on them after all."

"You think that's necessary?" Kyle's eyebrows furrowed.

"It may be if they continue to show up being belligerent and all as they have been."

"I'll do it if needed. I wish I could get a restraining order for Dennis to stay away from Karen."

Andrew burst out in laughter. "Man, you stupid."

"Man, if I could, I would in a heartbeat. He'd have to stay at least two million feet away from her. Matter of fact, I'd make the restraining order be so far away from her that he'd have to move to Africa to not violate it."

"Yeah, you'd love that, wouldn't you?" Andrew chuckled.

"Absolutely."

"You need to get ready to meet your daughter. Aww, how cute."

"Man, shut up." Kyle laughed. "What should I take her?"

"I don't know what little girls are into nowadays. A baby doll? Teddy bear?" Andrew shrugged his shoulders.

"Yeah, I'll grab a teddy bear on my way over."

"Good luck with meeting my niece, your daughter."

***

There was a knock at the door and Mercedes knew who was on the other side of it. She stared at her feet as one landed in front of the other until her hand touched the door knob. She took a deep breath and opened the door.

Kyle stood there with the hugest teddy bear she had ever seen. She thought it was cute.

"Hey. Come in." Mercedes pressed her lips tight trying to contain her laughter.

"What's funny?"

"That teddy bear you have. It's like three times as big as she is."

Kyle showcased a wide grin. "Well, I didn't know how tall she was or what to get her, so I grabbed the cutest thing I saw. You think she'll like it?"

"I think she'll love it. Come in. She's over there watching her favorite cartoon. Gabrielle, vir aqui, bebe."

"What?" Kyle's forehead scrunched.

Mercedes laughed. "I told her to come here."

"Oh, okay."

They stood there silently waiting for Gabrielle to come to the door.

"She hasn't come yet, so I guess we should go over to where she is. Sometimes I can't pry her away from the TV."

Kyle and Mercedes made their way over to the couch. At Kyle's expense, Mercedes decided to check into a suite at a hotel in the western suburbs of Chicago, trying to escape the media.

Mercedes offered Kyle a seat, but he could only stand and stare at the smaller girl version of himself. She had long, curly ponytails. He thought she was beautiful. Simply beautiful.

"Gabby, I want you to meet Kyle. Remember I told you that he's your father."

Gabby nodded her head slowly.

Mercedes continued talking knowing she already had explained to her daughter that she would meet Kyle, her father. "Kyle meet Gabrielle or Gabby as I call her."

Kyle squatted so that he could be eye level with Gabrielle. She stared at him with her big, soft brown eyes. She melted his heart. He knew that she would have him wrapped around her finger from that day forward.

"Hi." Gabby's voice squeaked.

Kyle smiled, choking on his tears. "Hi, Gabby. I have something for you." He pulled the big teddy bear from behind his back and her eyes lit up.

"Wow. That's big." Gabby smiled.

Kyle handed her the teddy bear. She tried to pick it up but fell back from the weight of it.

They all laughed.

Kyle managed to scoop her and the teddy bear up in one motion and put them on the couch setting the teddy bear down next to her.

"So, Gabby, you like the teddy bear?" Kyle asked,

"Yes. I love it. Olhe, mamae! Olhar!" Gabrielle pointed to the jewelry the teddy bear had on.

"Vejo, bebe, vejo," Mercedes said.

Kyle stared incredulously at Mercedes.

She laughed. "What? I'm Brazilian and speak Portuguese, so it's only right that she knows my native language, even if she's African American."

"You're right. It's just shocking to see such a little person be bilingual the way she is."

Kyle sat there staring at her little fingers. Listening to her little voice. *She's mine.* He didn't know before then that he could love someone so quick. Well, he knew that he loved Karen the moment that he met her. What he felt for Gabrielle was a special kind of love, a king watching over his princess kind of love.

Kyle managed to come up with questions to ask Gabby and she eagerly answered until she talked herself to sleep.

Kyle stared at her sleeping on the couch for a while. "Won't she hurt her neck slumping over like that if we leave her there?"

Mercedes laughed. "She'll be fine there. But yes, I should get her in bed now." Mercedes reached out to pick her up.

"Can I do it?"

"Sure."

Kyle gently pried Gabby's arms from around the teddy bear and laid her head on his shoulders. Still asleep, Gabby wrapped her little arms around Kyle's neck.

He sniffled.

Mercedes directed him to the bedroom. He stood next to the bed holding Gabby for quite some time before he decided to put her in the bed. He laid her down and tucked her in staring at her for as long as he could. He kissed her forehead and got up from the bed and quickly wiped away a tear. He didn't want Mercedes to see him cry.

She stood back in the shadow of the hallway as Kyle exited the room.

"Thank you for letting me see her."

"No problem. It was long overdue."

"Yeah." Kyle sighed.

"She seems to like you."

"Yeah." Kyle smiled. "I was nervous about how she would take to me, but I'm so glad everything worked out so far."

They walked towards the suite door.

"So when can I see her again?"

"It's up to you. I want you to have a relationship with her. I know that you're in the middle of the season and you'll be on the road. So I guess we can stay here in Chicago for a while so that you can see her when you're in town." Mercedes looked away. "I don't want her back and forth across the country as you travel. We'll go back to Miami soon, though."

Kyle frowned. "I want to be around her. I didn't even think about you all still living in Miami. Can we talk about you all possibly moving here?"

Mercedes was silent. She leaned against the door.

"I know I'll be here with the Bulls for at least three more years. I would like my daughter here with me. I have to get to know her. I want her to be comfortable with me and know that I love her. I want her to get to know my family, too, and they live here." Kyle's eyes pleaded with Mercedes.

"I'll think about it."

19

Karen tried her best not to keep up with Kyle via social media and all the gossip in the tabloids and blogs, but she couldn't help it. She just had to know what was going on with him.

She saw all the reports about him having come to an agreement with Mercedes Silva. She was glad that he would get joint custody of his daughter but was saddened that the little girl really was his. He had a child with another woman. Her heart sank.

She laid in bed thinking of how hard she tried to push him away in the beginning as long as she could, but ended up letting him into her heart, even when she thought that she hadn't.

They had talked about getting married and having children. His face lit up during those discussions, talking about how he wanted a little girl that would look just like her and a son that looked like him. She reminisced on the places they said they would take the kids and the extra-curricular activities they would enroll them in to make them cultured children. She realized she would never have that life with him.

She knew she had no choice but to move on with her life now, and that is what she was trying to do with Dennis. *He's a great guy. Any woman would be lucky to be with him.* He managed to fill in for Stacey King whenever he was sick or had a family emergency, which Karen admitted to herself had become frequent for Stacey since she started covering the games with him. His absences were unusual because he was present for all of the games in seasons past. However, this season with his frequent absences, Dennis was there to fill in for him and he made the best of each game they covered together.

It dawned on her that Dennis milked the situations by being extra flirtatious whenever Kyle looked at them, but she liked knowing that she was possibly making him jealous and wondering what he was missing out on.

Why does Kyle always pop up in my thoughts? Karen sighed.

She normally ran throughout the year, but it was winter and this particular morning was just too cold for her to go for a run. She was okay with not running because she relished the idea of staying in the comfort of her home before she had brunch with Dennis.

She had a game to cover that night, so she didn't want to be on the go every hour of the day.

The Bulls were playing the Spurs, the defending champions. She knew this would be a crucial game for them this season and wanted to be fully alert to report every second of the game and entertain the crowd.

As usual, she didn't hear a knock on the door, but she did hear a key twisting in the lock chamber. She knew it couldn't be anyone but Melanie. She buried herself under the covers pretending to be asleep, but before she knew it, an energetic body jumped across hers and landed on the other side of the bed.

"Why do you do that all of the time?" Karen mumbled from under the covers.

"Because I can and why are you still in bed? I know it's cold outside, but will you look at this?" Melanie jumped out of Karen's bed and opened the curtains. "It's such a beautiful day. The sun is shining and the sky is clear."

"I believe you. It's going to be even better when I see Dennis for brunch." She mustered up a smile.

"What?" Melanie snarled.

"Why the face? You still don't like him?"

Melanie turned from the window and jumped back into Karen's bed. "You know I don't." Melanie laughed. "Seriously, it's just that…" Melanie let her words trail off.

"Just what?"

"Nothing, never mind."

"I know what it is."

"What?" Melanie laughed.

"You want to say it's just that you wish that I was with Kyle, right?"

"Yeah," Melanie stated matter-of-factly. "I know I questioned you about thinking you had something so special with him after only a month or so, but the more I thought about it, I thought about Andrew and me. We made our connection within the first week, matter of fact, it was the first day we laid eyes on each other. You and Kyle were like that the first day you met on that run." Melanie laughed.

"Whatever."

"I saw it as you let your guard down with him in St. Lucia and especially when we came back. I want you with Kyle because you don't smile like that when you're with Dennis."

"What? I do, too."

"No, you don't."

"Whatever. Why must you always bring him up?"

"Because I just want you to be truly happy."

"I want to be happy, too, and I am happy with Kyle, I mean Dennis."

"I heard you say Kyle instead of Dennis and that's how I know you're not happy with him. 'Ms. Wordsmith', 'Ms. Journalist', you don't slip-up when it comes to words unless you mean it." Melanie tightened her mouth and cocked her head at Karen. "I want you to be truly happy. I don't want you to settle. Settle for someone who isn't even genuine. There's just something not right about him. I can feel it."

"So you're a physic now?" Karen's eyebrows raised in query.

"No, it's just like when you know, you know. And Dennis being wrong for you, that I know. He just doesn't rub me the right way." Melanie stared directly at Karen.

"Oh, so you think because you have this 'perfect' relationship with Andrew that you can give me advice and tell me who is and who isn't right for me?" Karen openly stared at Melanie.

"No. Me and Andrew's relationship is not perfect, just yet." Melanie laughed.

Karen pressed her lips tight trying to suppress a sarcastic response brewing in her.

"But that's beside the point. I wish you would stop acting like I don't know you. Like I said, you don't smile with Dennis the way you did with Kyle. The smile that you had with Kyle was from the depth of your soul. Meanwhile, the smile you have with Dennis is just the lifting up of the corners of your mouth. It's not from your heart, not in your eyes, nothing." Melanie shook her head.

"Oh shut up." Karen hit Melanie with a pillow.

Laughing, they continued to hit each other with pillows.

"Okay, you've made me tired. I need to take a quick nap before I get up and get ready."

"So where are you non-lovebirds off to today?"

"Ha ha, funny. We are going to have brunch at the Signature Room on the 95th floor over at the John Hancock Building."

"Mmph, that would be the perfect date with you know who."

Karen smiled. "Whatever. I'mma change my locks and kick you out of my life if you keep bringing him up. I'm not with Kyle, nor will I ever be with him again. He has a daughter. He'll probably get back with the mother of that daughter. He has two other crazy baby mommas as well."

"Assumed baby mommas."

"Whatever. I won't have diluted fantasies about being with him. I'm going to enjoy my time with Dennis and get to know him. Besides, I actually do like Dennis. I'm starting to care for him. He's such a great guy."

"Starting to? It was instantaneous with Kyle. Does he even make you feel any type of way Kyle did?

"Yep, even better. I don't question his loyalty."

"There you go again lying. You can keep lying to yourself, but you can't lie to me."

"Whatever. Get out so I can go back to sleep."

"I guess I'll leave you alone for now, but I'll see you tonight."

"Sorry, hun. I have a game to cover. No binging on ice cream and watching mushy love movies with my best friend tonight." Karen pouted.

"I know that's not on the menu tonight. Andrew got us tickets for the game." Melanie stuck her tongue out at Karen.

"Whatever. So I guess I will see you tonight."

"Is Stacey covering the game with you, or will Dennis magically be there broadcasting with you again tonight?"

"No, last time I checked Stacey will be there so the coverage should be really entertaining tonight. Although, I do have fun when Dennis is there, too. Thank you very much." Karen threw a pillow at

Melanie, but Melanie ducked and the pillow flew through the doorway into the hallway.

"Ha. You missed me. Talk to you later."

Karen laughed. "Okay, see you later."

***

Dennis leaned against his car outside of Karen's building.

"Hey, beautiful " He opened the car door for her, even though the concierge was there waiting to do the same.

She stood on her tiptoes and kissed him on the lips before she got in the car. He closed the door after her.

He was excited that she initiated physical contact with him. Maybe he really was getting to her. He rushed around to get out of the cold winter winds and jumped into the driver's seat. He sat for a second, looked at her, and went in to kiss her again.

She obliged him.

He tried to tongue kiss her, but she pulled back before he was allowed to deepen the kiss.

"Karen? You kissed me first just a minute ago. I thought that meant you really have warmed up to me. Are you still not comfortable with us?"

"No, it's not that." She turned to look out the passenger side window.

"So what is it?"

"I care about you, I just don't want to rush things with us. I don't want to do something that we can't undo. Get what I'm saying?"

"Yeah, I have no problem moving at your pace because that's just how much I want to be with you. So, we're staying at first base on our dates and I'm happy to be there. I'll even buy us popcorn while we're there." Dennis pulled off.

Karen's lips parted to respond to his quirky analogy but she decided against and fell silent as she sat in the car with him and they made their way to the Hancock Building in record time amidst the downtown traffic.

He paid valet to park his car and they headed to the elevator that would take them to the 95th floor. As they stood in line waiting to board the elevator, Karen felt Dennis's firm manhood as he nestled her to him with his hands around her waist. "What are you doing?" She leaned back and whispered in his ear.

"Oh nothing, just trying to keep you warm." He laughed.

"The heat is on in here." Karen turned around to face Dennis, but instinctively looked past him and stared into Kyle's eyes.

His gaze held hers as he stood behind her and Dennis.

I can't stay away from him. Out of all the places I could go on a date with Dennis, it had to be here where Kyle is with his new family. She looked down to see his hand gripping the hand of the adorable little girl she assumed to be his daughter. Her eyes traveled over to see the beautiful Mercedes Silva standing next to them. Karen tried not to show the disdain and sadness on her face, but she failed, as usual.

Kyle didn't want to stop looking into Karen's eyes. She was beautiful, and he couldn't help but to see the look on her face when she looked over at Gabby and Mercedes. He saw a look of sadness and hurt in her eyes.

The man controlling the elevators signaled for the next group to board. Karen had no choice but to get on the elevator with Kyle and his new family.

Dennis stood behind Karen at the back of the elevator and pulled her as close to him as possible.

Kyle stood directly next to them. He had a front row seat to the groping fest that Dennis was trying to engage Karen in. He noticed her struggling to keep a straight face, but her body squirmed under Dennis's touch. Kyle smiled.

"Kyle, Daddy, where are we going?" Gabby's voice rang out loud in the elevator.

Smiling, he looked down at her. "Remember, we're going to the restaurant at the top of this building. It has a pretty view of the city."

"Will Mommy see it, too?" Gabby stared into Kyle's eyes.

Karen's heart dropped.

Kyle smiled. "Yes, Gabby."

Karen tried her best to keep her tears at bay. She exhaled loudly when the elevator doors opened. She and Dennis were the last ones to exit the elevator.

"You go ahead to the table. I need to use the ladies room." She needed to compose herself. She rushed off to the bathroom grateful that no one else was in there as she leaned on the countertop tapping her nails. She let out a muted scream. *Why can't I ever escape this man?*

She stood up straight, smoothed out the sweater dress that hugged her in all the right places, and pushed her bang out of her face. She took a deep breath, exhaled, and headed to her table.

She spotted Dennis at their table before even having to ask the maitre'd where he was. She perked up walking towards him.

He stood and waited for her to sit before he took his seat again.

She tried smiling at him with her eyes as Melanie said she never did. She wanted to pull her mirror out to see if her eyes were actually smiling, but she looked past Dennis to see Kyle yet again.

He sat there smiling with his make-shift family.

She knew her eyes were not smiling at that point, and she didn't care if they weren't.

Dennis sensed the shift in Karen's mood. He figured it was due to Kyle's presence. He pulled out his phone and sent a quick text message to someone.

"You okay?" Dennis asked, trying to read Karen.

"It was good." Karen couldn't help but stare at Kyle and how affectionate and interactive he was with the adorable little version of himself. She cursed herself for thinking of how things would have been if that would have been her child that Kyle adored at that very moment.

"Karen? Karen?"

"Hunh?"

"We can go if you're not comfortable being here with Kyle and his family. Do you want to leave?

"No." Karen gathered her wits. "I'm sorry. Okay, I'm here now. See, I'm here." Karen put on a fake smile.

Dennis pulled out his phone again and messaged someone.

The waiter came and took their orders. That same waiter went over to Kyle's table and took his, Mercedes, and Gabrielle's orders.

Karen hated seeing the trio working together to give the waiter their orders.

Dennis tried to make Karen smile and laugh, but he just couldn't get the same emotions out of her that the sight of Kyle seemed to elicit from her. He pulled out his phone and texted someone again.

He managed to garner small talk out of her until their food arrived. They were halfway through their meals when there was a commotion behind him.

"Hey, Mr. Family Man. I see you all up in here with Pocahontas and your daughter. Yeah, buddy. I can't wait 'til this baby pop out and it's my turn for you to have me all up in fancy places like this with my daughter." Porsha rubbed her belly.

"Yeah, I don't even care if your wifey is with us with this little cutie." Unique pointed at Gabrielle.

The callous look Kyle gave Unique let her know that she needed to step back.

She did. "So, like I was saying, she can be here with this cutie. We should raise our kids together since they'll be brother and sisters."

"True," Porsha resounded.

Mercedes hung her head in shame as the two women continued to go back and forth about how they planned to exploit Kyle for all that he was worth.

Kyle stood up. Sheer anger and frustration laced his face. He was about to tear into the ladies with his words, but the maître-d intervened.

"Excuse me, ladies. I'm going to have to ask you all to leave."

"Why we gotta leave up out of here?" Porsha snapped.

"We can have lunch in here just like er'body else," Unique chimed in.

"No, you have to make reservations to do that. My apologies for whoever let you in without having a reservation, but we're going to have to ask you to leave immediately." He looked over at Kyle. "Sorry for the disturbance, Mr. Irving." He turned back towards the women. "Ladies." He extended his hand in front of him, signaling them to start walking.

They just stood there with their lips poked out and their hands on their hips.

The maitre'd nodded his head at the two burly security guards. They stepped forward and each one of them gently placed their arms around Porsha and Unique.

"Take your hands off of me," Unique barked.

"You can't put us out," Porsha shouted.

"This is some..." Unique belted out.

The guards remained stoic ignoring the women's threats and continued to escort them to the door.

Porsha and Unique continued threatening the men until they could no longer be heard in the restaurant.

Dennis tried his best to hide his smile from Karen.

"I'm so glad I avoided that."

"What?" Dennis pretended not to know what Karen was referring to.

"Having to deal with that circus of his life. Let's say we get out of here and go spend some alone time together before I have to go to the game tonight."

"That sounds like a great plan to me." Dennis helped her from her seat and they headed towards the door. He put his hand firmly around her waist, leaned in to her, and whispered, making her laugh as they walked out.

Kyle stared at them with contempt.

Gabrielle brought his attention back to the moment. "Daddy, who are those ladies?"

Kyle shook his head. "Don't worry about that, baby girl. Just some women you'll never be like when you get older."

Mercedes shook her head. She felt sorry for Kyle having to deal with those two women. She also could tell that he had a serious interest in the woman that stood in front of them while waiting for the elevator. That same woman that Kyle stared at on the elevator. The same woman who had just walked out with a man Kyle seemed to loathe.

20

Andrew lit candles and dimmed the lights. He wanted everything to be perfect for Melanie when she came over.

A knock at the door alerted him of her arrival.

"Mmmh, a goddess. Come in."

Melanie entered and Andrew quickly took her into his arms and kissed her madly.

"Andrew, let me get in the door first." She giggled.

"There's somewhere I want to get into." Andrew squeezed her butt.

They kissed until Melanie realized just how dark it was in Andrew's apartment. "What do you have going on in here? Why is it so dark?"

Andrew loosened his grip on Melanie so that she could look past him.

She saw that a feast was spread across the dining table. She gazed at him. "For me?"

"Of course for you. I would move the mountains and the heavens for you, so this was simple."

"Aww, thanks." She gave him a quick peck on his lips and walked past him to see what he had prepared for them.

He had made some of her favorites—grilled salmon, asparagus, garlic flavored mashed potatoes, and he even had strawberry cheesecake. He topped it off with her favorite wine, cabernet Sauvignon.

He stood behind her with his hands folded at his chest, admiring her slim waist, ample butt, and curvy hips. *Man, she is fine! I can't wait to get in to that tonight.* He pumped his fist in the air.

She turned towards him. Her eyes were dancing. "Thanks. This is so sweet of you."

"Come on." He led her to the table and pulled her chair out for her.

"It smells so good. I can't wait to eat."

They held hands and said grace, then immediately dug in. "I'm sorry for pigging out and eating so fast, but I was so hungry and this food is so good." She laughed. "I had a busy day at work."

"Oh really? Tell me about it."

"Yeah, I mean, the gallery is normally busy, but today was extremely busy. Apparently, there was an art buyer in town that had heard about my gallery in particular. He came and pretty much bought every piece I had. He even emptied out the storage room." She paused to take a bite of her salmon.

"We had to catalog all of the pieces he bought and secure shipping for them by next week." Melanie put a forkful of food into her mouth.

"But that's good for you, right?"

"Of course, but since I really don't have an inventory anymore I have to spend time finding more pieces to restock the gallery. But that shouldn't be a problem because I've come across a great new artist that I'm dying to get his work into the gallery."

"Well, that sounds good." Andrew stared at Melanie gobbling her food. He silently laughed.

"And what about your day?"

"My day was straight. I closed some deals for a few clients. Of course I'm still trying to deal with the issues with the women with Kyle. Since they haven't had the kids yet, they're being a nuisance because we can't legally prove if the kids are his or not. I need to get them out of our hair ASAP." Andrew huffed.

"Get them out of your hair? That sounds rude."

"I'm sorry. I don't mean it like that, but they are beasts in contrast to Mercedes. She's so nice. She's not looking to come up on Kyle, she just wants him to have a relationship with Gabrielle. She doesn't even trip about money. Of course, she's grateful that Kyle gives her enough money a month not only to take care of Gabrielle, but so that she can live comfortably, too."

"Oh." Melanie gave him a look letting him know to keep talking.

"She didn't come forward for the money. Whereas the other two, I don't want to call them chickenheads, even though that's the way they act like. Oh, what the hell. Those two chickenheads are just so eager to use these babies to get money and fame by having his kids."

"Yeah, I get that from them, too, but that's what happens when you just go to bed with anyone."

"Yeah, that'll never happen between us. I know what we have between us is strong. I can't wait to make you my wife and for us to have beautiful chocolate kids together just like you and I." Andrew smiled and reached for Melanie's hand.

She pulled back from him. "Andrew."

"What? What? I brought up marriage again? I brought up wanting to have kids with you again? I'm sorry, Melanie, but you've known I've felt this way about you pretty much since the beginning. Whether we talk about it or not, you know the connection between us is strong and there's more for us than just spending lots of time with each other. We're meant to be more than just friends. I thought you felt that way, too?" Andrew's eyebrows raised.

"I do, it's just that…" Melanie sighed and put her head in her hands.

Andrew rubbed her knees. "What's wrong, Melanie?"

She looked up at him. "I know I shouldn't let my past dictate my future and as an adult I'm responsible for my ways of thinking, no matter what I was taught as a kid, but some lessons I haven't gotten over yet. I hold onto many because they are valuable, and then there are some I need to let go of because they aren't conducive to what I want to be in life or where I'm trying to go." She signed. "There are just certain things that my mom always told me growing up about men—"

Andrew interrupted her. "Like what?"

"The amount of trust that I should put in them. That has stuck with me and always made me kind of skeptical about moving forward with a man."

"What do you mean? You've never really talked about your mom all these months. I've asked about meeting her, getting to know her, and you always avoid the subject. I should've figured she had something to do with you not trusting me." Andrew dropped his fork, leaned back into the chair, and rubbed his forehead.

She was sweating. "It's not that I don't trust you. I mean, your day to day actions show me that I can trust you. I believe I can trust you. I feel I can trust you. It's just that you're so ready for marriage and kids and I can't say that I'm ready to give you that. Not just because of me, but I have to take my mom's feelings into consideration."

Andrew sat up straight in the chair. "Melanie, stop talking in circles."

"I don't know how to explain her." Melanie placed her fork on the table and pushed her plate away from her.

"Try. Why don't you let me meet your mom and then maybe once she gets to know me, she'll see that all men aren't the same. She'll see I'm one of the good guys, that I'm good for you, and then maybe you'll be comfortable moving forward with me."

"Drew, we talked about this before." Melanie sighed.

"Yeah, I know, I know, I know. I can't meet her. And you won't tell me exactly why." Andrew rubbed his face in frustration. He tried to perk up, remembering he had plans for her body that night. He wanted to get her in the mood. "I'll leave it alone, for now." He grimaced. He pulled her up from the table, wrapped his arms around the small of her back, and planted kisses all over her neck.

"Thanks."

She fell limp in his arms as his lips made their way over her body.

Andrew could tell that she was ready to take it to the next level with him. He guided her over to the couch.

Floetry's "Yes" was playing in the background.

All you gotta do is say yes, don't deny what you feel let me undress you baby, open up your mind and just rest, I'm about to let you know you make me so...

The mood was just right.

He slowly laid her on the couch and spread her legs with his knees as he climbed on top of her. He kissed her from her chin down to the opening of her shirt and began to squeeze her breasts and made circular motions with his pelvis against her.

She moaned in ecstasy. "Drew. Don't stop."

Her screams gave him clearance to go further. He opened her blouse and nibbled on her breasts through her bra. He slid his finger under her skirt.

Her phone rang.

"Don't answer it, baby." He moaned.

"No, I have to. That's my mother's ringtone."

Andrew huffed and allowed her to move to get the phone from the coffee table.

"Hi, Mom…What?...Now?...Okay. I'll be there in a sec." Melanie knew that her mother was having another one of her episodes and she was the only one that could calm her down.

Andrew's eyes bucked wide open. "Hunh? You have to go now?"

"Yes, I'm sorry. I have to."

"Melanie." Andrew took a deep breath. "Every time we get to this point, your mom calls and you have to rush out."

"I can't talk about it now. I'll fill you in some other time." Melanie buttoned her blouse and put her shoes and coat on. "I have to go. Bye." She rushed out the door.

Andrew was frustrated. He loved Melanie, but he was tired of the secrecy surrounding her mom. He knew he needed to get to the bottom of it and soon.

21

It was well after All-Star weekend and the Bulls were a shoe-in to be the Eastern Conference Champions. They were in Toronto playing against the Raptors.

Kyle had spent as much time as he could with Gabrielle. He even convinced Mercedes to let Gabrielle travel to some of the cities he played in to spend as much time with her as possible. He invited Mercedes to go on the road with them but she always declined. She thought it would be best if she didn't travel with them since the tabloids were still set on making them a couple, even though they weren't. Mercedes and Kyle agreed on a nanny for Gabrielle to travel with her on the road and take care of her as needed. There could be no mistaking from the older woman's attire and demeanor that she wasn't Kyle's new love interest, but merely someone who tended to Gabrielle while he played.

While many of his other teammates partied all night in clubs and in their hotel rooms, Kyle made sure that his room was on the other side of the hotel, away from all the noise, so that he could spend quality time alone with Gabrielle.

Kyle was in Toronto and he knew who he could have a good time with—Veronica. He met her the last time he was there and figured it would be a great idea to see her again. He wasn't looking for someone new because he didn't necessarily want to get over Karen, but he figured he would have to at some point. She always seemed so chummy with Dennis every time he saw them together. He hated how Dennis made it a point to put his hands all over Karen, signaling to everyone, especially him, that they were an item.

If Karen could move on so easily, maybe he could, too. Veronica's success attracted her to him. She didn't seem like she wanted him for his money, and he thought she had a banging body, so he didn't have any problems with spending time with her. If anything, she would help take his mind off Karen.

It was Friday night before the game and the players had to be in town to make sure there would be no delays in their arrivals for the game on Saturday night.

Gabrielle stayed behind with her mom, so he came in early Friday morning for practice and because he wanted to spend some time with Veronica. They had been talking for a little over a month, but because of the Bulls' tight schedule and her busy schedule, they had to resort to getting to know each other via the video app Tango, as well as texting and phone calls.

Veronica arranged to take Kyle out and show him around her hometown. Toronto was beautiful and they would explore its splendor soon enough, but she wanted to take him to see Niagara Falls first.

"I'm so glad you could meet me tonight. How has everything been going?" Veronica smiled at Kyle as they headed down Queen Elizabeth's Way to Niagara Falls.

"Everything's been going great. My team is definitely coming out of the east. I love my daughter. I love spending time with her."

"Glad to hear life is good for you now." Veronica smiled.

Kyle stared out the window thinking on how his life wasn't as good as he wanted it to be because Karen wasn't in it.

"Are you okay?"

"Yeah." Kyle smirked. "Why'd you ask that?"

She shrugged her shoulders. "You just had this lost-in-translation look on your face."

Kyle laughed nervously. "Naw, I'm just looking out the window. That's all."

"Enjoying the scenery, hunh?"

Kyle struggled to get comfortable in the back seat with his legs being so long. He turned trying to get more comfortable and ended up completely facing her. "Yeah, that's it. Canada is beautiful. Your city is beautiful. You know I've been here before for games but never really had the time or desire to really explore it, until now. With you."

Veronica blushed.

"The best part about this trip here is that I get to look at this beautiful woman and enjoy Niagara Falls with her."

"I wonder who this woman is that you speak of. She must be lucky if she gets a chance to be with the handsome Kyle Irving and enjoy his company." Veronica batted her eyes at Kyle.

The scenery was breathtaking to both of them. Their hands met and intertwined as they rode in silence until they reached Niagara Falls. They made it there, grabbed their raincoats, and started their descent down the falls.

Kyle stood next to Veronica and made small talk, leaning over to whisper in her ear as needed because the roaring sounds of the water overpowered their conversation much of the time.

***

Karen was excited that Dennis had flown up to Toronto to spend some time with her. However, she was annoyed that of all the places they could choose to have a date she would have to endure Kyle all hugged up with another woman, and it wasn't even Mercedes.

Her heart kept betraying her. She was with Dennis so she didn't understand why her heart couldn't catch up with that fact. She turned to face Dennis. "I'm so glad you came up to visit me this weekend."

"You know I would come anywhere around the world to see you."

"You do know the next game is Monday night in Chicago? I would've been back home by Sunday eve."

"Yeah, I know, but I just couldn't go that long without seeing you. Besides, I love Canada. I figured it would be a great place for us to spend more quality time together outside of you working Saturday night."

"I like how you think." She laid her head on his chest and held on tightly to him. She tried to block out images of Kyle being all cozy with the woman unknown to her. She needed to talk her heart out of still loving him.

Dennis loved Karen being as close to him as she was. He held on as tight to her as he possibly could. He smiled.

He was enjoying the moment until he looked up and saw Kyle staring at him. *I'm sick of this man. Ha! I hope he enjoys this.* He looked down at Karen.

The mist from the rush of the falls seemed to be tickling her pert little nose as she kept rubbing it. She smiled and squirmed in his arms in delight as she swatted at the mist as if she could make it disappear from around her.

The splendor of the Niagara Falls was a worthy sight to see, but Karen was a treasured vision to him. He longed for her to look at him the way he looked at her, but he could tell her feelings for him didn't match his just yet. *I have to work my plan harder.*

The calming but loud rush of the water landscaping the falls roared around them as he grabbed her chin and caressed her lips with his. He soon devoured her with a kiss and held her tightly. He relaxed against the guard rail behind him and grabbed her bottom and kissed her deeper and deeper, stealing moments away from the kiss and looking through the mist to see if Kyle was still looking at him.

The scour on Kyle's face let him know that he was furious.

Dennis grabbed Karen's bottom even harder and continued to kiss her until she pulled back from him.

"Dennis, what's gotten into you?" She pushed her wet hair out of her face.

"Nothing." He laughed. "I've always wanted to kiss you like this." He kissed her again and smiled.

Karen's lips curved up before she spoke. "Well, we can't keep this up with those kids over there staring at us." Karen shook her head and pointed to the teenagers laughing near them.

"We can if we take this back to the hotel. That's if you want?"

Karen thought for a second. "What the hell." She grabbed his hand. "Come on, let's go." She pulled him as he looked back smiling at Kyle.

***

Karen tried to get into the moment at the hotel, but she just couldn't bring herself to have sex with Dennis yet. She knew her feelings were still too strong for Kyle to share herself physically with Dennis. She didn't want sex with Dennis to further cloud her emotions between the two men. Although she did find it strange that she had been committed to being Dennis's girlfriend, but couldn't confess to loving him or having sex with him, yet.

***

The game was just about to start and Karen was glad that it would be a distraction for her. She definitely needed Stacey's banter to take her mind off things that happened earlier that day. She could tell that Dennis was frustrated with not having sex, but at the same time he seemed to be okay waiting until she was ready to take their relationship to that level. He was such a great man. She wondered if she would ever be able to totally give her heart to him.

"Karen, so what do you think about tonight's matchup? The Bulls up against the number one ranking Toronto Raptors."

"Well, Stacey, the Raptors have been playing great this entire year, but so have the Bulls. No other team in the league has the depth that the Bulls have. They have really been playing defense. They've prevented their opponents from scoring more than eighty points in the last ten games. Their offense has been firing on all cylinders, too. I think this is going to be a great game."

"It definitely will be, especially with Kyle Irving being on fire since All-Star break."

"Yeah, he has." Karen inwardly laughed at her fake enthusiasm when mentioning Kyle. If he listened to the playback of the game, she didn't want to give him the impression that she would welcome his presence back in her life, but she still wanted to sound impartial about him seeing as though she was a commentator.

"Yes. The Bulls were a great team before he got here, but he's definitely proven to be quite an asset. He's worth what they paid for him."

"Well, we just want to win a championship. Maybe the odds are in our favor." They continued to make comments as the game got underway.

Two quarters passed and the teams were tied going into halftime.

Stacey excused himself from the table and Karen was left with her meddling thoughts. She thought about how Gabrielle was at many of the games during the season and smiled recounting never seeing Mercedes. She figured that meant Mercedes and Kyle were not a couple, or were at least trying not to give that impression. She assumed the woman who kept Gabrielle during the games wasn't Kyle's love interest because she looked more like she could be his mother or aunt in age. But she figured the woman bore no relation to him seeing as though she was white.

The players on both teams came back onto the floor to shoot around.

Karen looked up to see a beautiful woman sitting on the sidelines and Kyle staying near her, dribbling the ball as they chatted. The woman was smiling wide at whatever he was saying to her. He really was making her laugh. *How fake!*

Karen could tell from the way the woman looked at Kyle that she was really into him. He was giving her enough of his attention during his shoot around time to suggest that he must like her as well.

How long have they known each other? Are they dating? Have they had sex yet? Is that any of my business? Uggghhhh. I need to focus on opening my heart to Dennis and not sulking over Kyle. Dennis is such a great guy. He deserves more of me than what I've been giving him. She was lost in thought staring at Kyle and the woman.

The buzzer sounded, signaling the players that the game would resume.

She looked up and locked eyes with Kyle. His stare was penetrating. She became unnerved under it. She turned her head and pretended to talk to the sports announcer from another network next to her until she felt Kyle's stare dissipate.

Stacey returned and they continued commenting on the game. They went back and forth about how each player was performing and how the coaches were responding to the various fouls their players received.

The Bulls went on a 12-0 run from the beginning of the quarter and gave themselves a twenty-point lead.

The Raptors tried, but they could never manage to get the lead again throughout the remainder of the game.

The Bulls won by twelve points with Kyle being the most dominant player during the game. Karen had no choice but to interview him seeing as though the regular interviewer had to be rushed off right after the game.

"So, Kyle, how does it feel to be the Bulls leading scorer for the night?" She tried her best to keep her distance from him but because the crowd was still loud, she had to draw close to him to be heard and hear him.

"I mean it feels great to be a part of this organization. My teammates have really helped me fit into Thibbs' system. They trust that if they pass me the ball when I'm open, I'll make the shot. It's not about me though, it's about us working together to win these games. To win the championship. We're coming for you Spurs." Kyle laughed, looking straight into the camera.

"Wow, that's such a bold statement. So you think that you all can take the Spurs this year?" She put the mic back in his face.

"Of course. There's no contesting the fact that the Spurs are a great pain for any team, but what the Bulls have this year is special. We definitely want to bring another ring, another banner back to the United Center, the madhouse on Madison."

"Well, if you all keep playing the way you do then that might be a reality for my hometown." Karen smiled. "Now back to you in the studio."

The cameramen went away and Karen stood there as a crew member detached the mic cords from her.

Kyle hung around to speak to her. "So, how have you been?"

"I'm doing good." She smoothed her hair down.

"I see you're definitely holding it down over there. We don't get a chance to hear all of what you say, but Andrew tells me that you and Stacey are hilarious."

"Yeah, I mean it's definitely not me that's the funny one. I just feed off Stacey. He's the best."

"Yeah, he is funny, but you definitely have a great sense of humor, too. You kept me laughing days after you said something." Kyle smiled, looking into her eyes.

She held his stare.

Veronica made her way across the court and locked her elbow with Kyle's.

Kyle hated to break his stare from Karen's, but he figured he had to give his attention to Veronica. He looked to his right. "Oh, hey, Veronica. Veronica, this is Karen, Karen this is my friend, Veronica."

Veronica smiled at Karen. She extended her hand to shake Karen's.

Karen stared at the model-like hand before she faked a more brilliant smile and shook Veronica's hand.

"Hi, Karen. I love your work as a broadcaster. You crack me up whenever I get the chance to watch the game."

"Thanks." Karen tried to mask any jealousy in her voice. *Why should I be jealous or upset? I'm the one who told him to move on with his life and that I didn't want anything to do with him. I have a great man back at the hotel waiting on me.*

"Well, good game, Kyle. You two enjoy the rest of your evening." Karen pivoted and subtly swayed her hips as she walked away. Once out of their sight, she rushed back to her hotel. She would no longer allow her feelings for Kyle to hold her back. She was ready to move forward with Dennis.

22

Karen couldn't believe that she and Dennis had been a couple for the past six months. Things seemed to be going really well for them. She knew in the beginning she kept her guard up with him because she had not dealt with her true feelings for Kyle, but she felt like she was over Kyle and had really opened up to Dennis. She gave him the attention that he deserved from her.

Things had changed dramatically for them since that weekend in Toronto. She had went back to the hotel that night and really let her guard down with him. They shared a very erotic encounter. Karen knew she loved him, she just wasn't sure if she was in love with him. There were times when she would see Kyle at a game with that all too familiar stare at Veronica and it pulled on her heart. She worked hard to dismiss the feelings rising in her. She surmised it was just residual jealousy for him and not that she was still in love with him. She would immediately go see Dennis after the game if he were in town and would be intimate with him, trying to get Kyle out of her head, but more importantly, her heart.

***

Dennis thought he had Karen right where he wanted her, fully trusting in him. He worked hard day by day to prove to her that he was the man for her. He showered her with his attention and gave her gifts as he saw fit. She never had to worry about women claiming that he fathered their children. He was a perfect gentleman to her, in his eyes.

***

It was date night for Karen and Dennis, and she stood in her bathroom getting ready. As usual, Melanie came over to chat with her.

Melanie pranced into the master bathroom smelling of her familiar coconut oil. "Hey, girl. I see you're getting ready, but for what, another date with Dennis?" Melanie scrunched her nose.

Karen laughed. "Yes, I'm going out with my boo."

"Your boo?"

"Yeah, my boo."

"Only the youngin's can say boo. At our age, either a man is courting us for marriage or he's already our husband. We don't have time for games or that high school 'girlfriend-boyfriend' stuff."

"Yeah, you're right. But your man can still be your boo if he treats you right." Karen winked.

"Anywho, I see your dresses keep getting shorter and shorter." Melanie laughed.

"Well, it is getting warmer and warmer." Karen winked.

"Stop with all the winking. Jeesh."

Melanie raised her hands in protest. "I just want to look good for my man."

"You look good in anything with those runners legs. Speaking of running, do you still run into Kyle when you're out there in the mornings?"

"Well, you would know the answer to that if you ran with me anymore. But you spend so much of your time with Andrew now. I guess he took over as your new running mate." Karen pouted.

"I'm sorry about that, girl. But yeah, he does take up a lot of my time."

"I may have seen him once or twice over these past months," Karen said.

"And what happened when you saw him? Don't leave out anything."

"Nothing."

"What do you mean nothing?"

"Yeah, I said nothing. We look at each other, maybe wave to one another, but that's it."

"What kind of look?"

Karen laughed. "What do you mean what kind of look? The kind of look two people give each other when they acknowledge each other's presence."

"Again, you're talking to someone that knows you." Melanie raised her eyebrows, staring at Karen. "What kind of look do you give each other?"

Karen wondered if she should be totally honest with Melanie. She decided she might as well because she knew Melanie would see right through a lie. She sighed. "I guess we give each other that 'I miss you, but I've moved on because I see that you've moved on' look."

"Wow. That's deep."

"Well, whatever. I'm here getting ready to go out with Dennis." Karen smiled.

"You said 'Dennis' as if you've been getting down and dirty with him?"

"Well..." Karen's eyes danced.

"Karen. You're kidding, right? You haven't had sex with Dennis already, have you?"

"What? I didn't say I did."

"You didn't have to say anything. It's written all over your face. You don't have to say a word," Melanie sing-said it to the melody of the old school Rude Boys song.

"Okay, yes. I have sex with my boyfriend." Karen leaned against the bathroom countertop and focused on her reflection in the mirror as she patted her short do. "There is nothing wrong with me being with him in that way. *Aside from us not being married.* I'm sure you and Andrew have had plenty more sex together than Dennis and I have."

"No." Melanie turned her back to Karen. She went into the walk-in closet and rummaged through the clothes.

Karen bucked her head and rushed to Melanie. "What? Are you saying that you and Andrew haven't had sex yet?"

"No. We haven't." Melanie tried on a pair of Karen's shoes.

"Why not? Why the heck not? Remember, you two have this 'uncanny chemistry', so why not explore every facet of it?"

"Girl, I've tried." Melanie blew out a long sigh in frustration. "Trust me, we try, but I kid you not, every single time we're almost at the point of having sex, I mean with his hands and lips all over me, my mother always calls needing me. It's like she knows exactly when to call and stop my fun." Melanie plopped down on the floor of the spacious closet.

Karen joined her. "Does she be having one of her episodes when she calls you?"

"Yes, girl. She honestly was having one every single time he and I were about to go there. It's so frustrating for me, so I know it's incredibly frustrating for him. But you know that I have to go be there with her. I've learned over the years that I'm the only one that can calm her down when she gets like that." Melanie played with the buckles on a pair of Jimmy Choo's.

"So she still hasn't told you anything about why she gets like that?"

"Nope."

"Has she ever come clean as to why she's talked down about men to you all of these years?"

"Not that either. I don't even ask her anymore. I tried so much when I was a teenager and especially in my early twenties to get it out of her, but I've just come to accept the fact that she may never explain it to me."

219

"Would you stop rearranging my shoes?" Karen laughed. "And none of your aunts can tell you what happened either?"

"Well, you know there are only two of them and sadly enough, my mom doesn't talk to them. She's distanced herself from her family."

"Still, have you tried asking them about it?"

"Yes. I've talked to them about it quite a few times and they told me it was nothing that happened in the house while they were growing up because they had loving parents. They were extremely close growing up so if something was done to her, she would have come to them and told them. Plus, their brother was overprotective, like a hawk watching over them. They just don't believe it's something that happened in the house when she was a little girl."

"Wow. All these years she's told you about how untrustworthy men are and she's had the episodes and you still don't know why. Glad that didn't jade your perception of men." Karen said the last part sarcastically.

Melanie's eyes shifted. "I'm not jaded. My father was around. He helped to balance out my viewpoint of men, even though it didn't work between my mom and him."

"Balance it out?"

"Just like me, you haven't always been so willing to trust men, either. And it's not that I didn't really trust them, I was afraid to go all in with them only for it not to work out because of the way my mom might react to me having a man. I would have to tell her about him, introduce him to her at some point."

"I guess." Karen rubbed her fingers through the soft carpet. "Have you ever asked your dad what happened with your mom?"

"Yeah, but he doesn't know either. He said when he met her, he knew it was something different about her. She seemed withdrawn from life, but it was that same mystique that drew him to her. He said she didn't open up much to him about her past. He said he learned just enough about her to make him love her."

"So, what happened between them?"

"He tried to make it work with her as long as possible, but as time went on she became more and more withdrawn from him to the point that he felt it was best if they not be together anymore, just work together to focus on raising me. I guess I didn't turn out as bad as I could have, considering my mom and being your best friend and how you're so untrustworthy of men." Melanie laughed.

Karen swatted at Melanie.

"Whatever. It's not that I don't trust men, I just don't trust certain types of men."

"Listen to how you said that as if you still have feelings for a certain someone."

"Watch it." Karen pointed at Melanie. "Anyway, let me finish getting ready for my date with my boyfriend, Dennis Michaels, whom I love very much." Karen got up from the closet floor and went back to the bathroom counter top.

Melanie followed her.

"So are you in love with him?"

"What?"

"You heard me. Are you in love with him?"

"Hello. I just said I love him."

"There's a difference between loving someone and being in love with him."

"Okay, Ms. Know-It-All. Why don't you tell me what the difference is then?" Karen put her hands on her hips, waiting to hear what Melanie had to say.

"Nope. I'll let you think about it for a while and the next time we talk, you can tell me what the difference is. I'll give you a hint, think about how you feel about Kyle versus how you feel about Dennis. I bet Dennis would never leave twenty million dollars behind for you like Kyle did." Melanie tried to leave but Karen grabbed her wrist.

"Wait, what are you talking about?"

"You're the one into sports. I thought you knew."

"Knew what?"

"That's right. Kyle didn't let them disclose the exact amounts to the public, but the Clippers offered him twenty million more than the Bulls did."

"That doesn't mean anything. Players take pay cuts all the time to join teams they think have the best chance at winning the championship."

"That may very well be true, but I have the inside scoop."

"Oh really? And what's that?"

"Kyle didn't care how little the Bulls were going to offer him as long as he was able to join them. And before you say it, I know that the Bulls are set to take it all, but Kyle was more interested about being in Chicago to be with you."

Melanie left Karen wide-eyed and slack-jawed.

***

Karen found it strange that Dennis asked her to meet him out at Buckingham Fountain. He normally picked her up for their dates. But it didn't bother her because the location wasn't too far from her house. The cab ride there would give her a chance to breathe and enjoy the scenery of Michigan Avenue en route to the fountain on the gorgeous spring evening.

She made it to the fountain earlier than Dennis and sat on a bench staring at those around her. She focused her attention on an older couple seated nearby. They were holding hands staring at one another as the radiance of the sun setting provided an ethereal backdrop for them. The body language between them spoke volumes; they were still madly in love with one another.

She hoped that she could have that someday at that age with the love of her life. *Do I know the difference between loving a man and being in love with him? Of course I do. I'm too old not to know that by now. I know how love feels. Dennis is dependable and responsible. He has everything that a man could offer a woman. That's enough to love him, right?*

There was darkness and she realized that someone had their hands over her eyes. She would have been scared had she not picked up on the scent of his cologne. She turned around. "Dennis?"

He covered her lips with his before he took his hands off her. "Hey, beautiful. How are you?"

"I'm great. So is this our date? No food, no dancing, just Buckingham Fountain?" Karen pouted.

"Don't be in such a rush." Dennis laughed. "The night is young. We can do all of those things if you want to." He kissed her again.

He engaged her in conversation as the rustling of people around them became louder. Dennis held Karen's stare until she heard someone yell, 'Hit it.' She looked to the right of her to see a young man pecking at the keyboard before he started singing John Legend's "All of Me". He sounded great.

'Cause all of me
Loves all of you
Love your curves and all your edges
All your perfect imperfections
Give your all to me
I'll give my all to you
You're my end and my beginning
Even when I lose I'm winning
Cause I give you all of me
And you give me all of you, oh

Dennis spun her around to see all of the action. He pulled her closer to him and wrapped his arms around her waist. She interlaced her fingers with his.

A young woman appeared out of nowhere, twirling in a white, long, flowing skirt. She stopped short of Karen and began to sing "Angel" by the sultry songstress Anita Baker. The woman's voice rang out loud among the crowd.

If I could, I'd give you the world
Wrap it all around you
Won't be satisfied with just a piece of his heart
My angel
Oh, angel
You're my angel
Oh, angel

Dennis squeezed Karen tighter. "I love you."

The man who had sung and played the John Legend song began singing with the woman. They blended so well.

Karen was excited to hear them perform more.

Dennis moved hastily behind her. She didn't bother to turn to see what he was doing because another man appeared out of nowhere and began singing another one of her favorite songs. Stevie Wonder's "Ribbon In The Sky"

Oh, so long before this night I prayed
That a star would guide you my way
To share with me this special day...
If allowed, may I touch your hand
And if pleased may I once again?
So that you too will understand...
This is not a coincidence
And far more than a lucky chance
But what it is that was always meant
There's a ribbon in the sky for our love

Karen mouthed the words of the song as they

continued to sing. She sensed that Dennis was no longer behind her. She immediately turned to see where he was and looked up in awe at the banner in the sky, waving from a small airplane. It said, *Will you marry me?*

She was confused. She saw the sign but not Dennis. She felt someone tug on her hand and she looked down to see Dennis on bended-knee with an open ring box. The diamond on the ring was huge.

The sun had fully set, but the lights from the fountain and the sound of the water hitting the fountain basin provided a magical ambiance for the moment.

Karen held her breath. *Is this really happening? To me?*

"Karen, I've loved you from the moment that I met you. I knew that I had to build a friendship with you before I tried to be your man. It's been a slow journey, but I wouldn't trade a second of it for the world. I'm so grateful that you gave me the opportunity to be your man, your lover. You are the best thing that has ever happened to me, and I don't want to go another moment without knowing that you'll give me the honor of being my wife. I want to start a family with you. I want us to travel the world together as husband and wife. Karen Charice Roberts, I love you so much and I need to know right now, at this moment, will you do me the honor of being my wife?" Dennis stared into her eyes.

"Dennis, Dennis, I... you're a great man. You've been so patient with me. You've shown me that you love me time and time again, and I thank you for that." Her eyes widened with shock. "This is so sudden. I don't know what to say." She put her hands up to her face.

"Just say you'll marry me, baby. Say that you'll do me the honor of being my wife."

Karen thought hard. *Do I only just love him or am I in love with him?* She thought about all the moments that they shared together. The conversations they had. *Wait, I would be a fool not to marry this wonderful, fine man in front of me.* "Yes, I'll marry you." She flashed him a smile.

He jumped to his feet and kissed her passionately until he realized that he had not put the ring on her finger yet. He pulled back from her, placed it on her finger, and resumed kissing her will all of his might as the crowd around them clapped loudly.

23

Andrew tried to wrap his head around the fact that every time he and Melanie were at the point of having sex, her mother always managed to call and Melanie had to rush out to tend to her. He didn't understand what the issue was. He often asked Melanie if he could go with her to help, but she quickly turned him down and rushed out.

He would make sure tonight he found out exactly what was going on with Melanie and her mother that kept them from going to the next level in their relationship.

He took a deep breath and knocked on her door.

"Just a minute." Melanie opened the door and all Andrew could do was smile. She was so beautiful.

He didn't want to make her upset, but he had to have this conversation with her. He loved her so much and was eager to further their relationship to the highest level—marriage. It didn't matter to him if they had only known each other less than a year. He knew what his heart was saying.

If he had to, he could do without having sex with her until they got married, but he definitely felt like he had to meet her family before they got married, especially considering he didn't know his biological parents. He was big on family and wanted to be comfortable with hers before he made that final commitment to a woman.

"Come in." She grabbed the bouquet of flowers from him and pulled him in with her free hand.

He closed the door with his foot.

She made her way to the kitchen, found a vase, and put water and the flowers in it.

He was on her heels and as soon as she turned around, she fell into his embrace. They kissed fervently, heaving and breathing heavily.

"Your lips taste so good. I bet something else tastes good, too." Andrew winked.

"You're so silly." She hit him on his shoulder. "Are you hungry?"

He rubbed his hands together and raised his eyebrows rapidly. "Of course."

She knew he wasn't talking about the food that she had prepared. "Would you stop being mannish? Come on, I want to feed you."

"I want you to feed me, too." He made a sopping sound.

"Drew, stop being so nasty. Come on." She led him to the table and sat him down. She went back over to the countertop and grabbed the plates she already prepared for them. She sat his food in front of him.

"This smells and looks good. Come on, let's hurry up and eat so I can get to dessert."

She pursed her lips and squinted her eyes. "Let's eat the food on our plates first." She laughed and sat down.

He grabbed her hand and they said grace before they dug into the food.

They were pretty much done eating when Andrew decided to broach the subject of Melanie's mom again. "Babe?"

"What?" Melanie smiled lovingly at Andrew as she always did.

"Guess what's coming up pretty soon in a couple of months?"

"What?"

"Our anniversary." Andrew said.

"Our anniversary?"

"Yeah. We've pretty much been exclusive since the first day we met each other down in St. Lucia, so I would say that it's coming up to our one-year anniversary."

Melanie squeaked. "Yeah, I guess so, hunh?"

He repositioned his chair to be directly in front of her, grabbed her by both hands, and stared into her eyes. "Melanie Daniels, what we have between us is real. I know that I want to spend the rest of my life with you. I think the perfect one-year anniversary gift to me would be that you marry me." He searched her eyes for agreement.

Melanie's mouth was dry. "Huh? Marry you?" She gulped air.

"Yes, marry me."

"Is this a proposal?" Melanie was stunned.

"No, it's a conversation. For as much as I want to marry you, I can't do that until we have met the most important people in each other's lives, and for you that's your mother."

Melanie threw her head back and sighed loudly. "Drew, we've been through this before. It's not a good time for you to meet my mom now."

"But when will it ever be? At first you told me that you didn't want to introduce me to her until you knew for sure that you loved me. You've confessed that you love me. You almost sound like you were going to say yes to that 'proposal'." Andrew laughed. When will there ever be a good time to meet your mom?"

"Drew, honestly, I don't think it ever will be a good time for you to meet her." Melanie pulled her hands out of his. She put her head down and rubbed her forehead.

He cupped her chin and lifted her face to look into her eyes. "Melanie, you can talk to me about it. You can talk to me about anything. What's going on? Is your mom sick and you don't want me to see her? You think I'll pity her? Pity you? What is it, baby? Just talk to me."

Melanie averted eye contact with him, leery of the subject matter. "No, she's not sick. She's physically fine. She's just emotionally damaged to the point that when I was in love in my early twenties, she berated me about the relationship. I figured once she met him she would see that he was a great guy and let up on me being with him."

"Did she?"

"No. I took him to meet her and she went absolutely berserk. I mean, she literally tore up the entire house. Smashing every mirror and anything else breakable she could get her hands on. We had to replace so much stuff. She functioned before that day, but since then, she's totally withdrawn from the world and has these weird episodes often. After that, I knew it wouldn't be a good idea for me to bring a man around her ever again until she got better, and judging from her frequent episodes, she's not better."

"Why do you think she's that way?"

"People who know about her episodes always ask me that question, but I have no answer and that frustrates and hurts me. It's just something that she won't talk to me about. Whatever it is has shaped the way she's talked to me about men. I talk to my family about it to try to find out more information. Even my dad couldn't say what it was that made her go off, but just added to why they couldn't be together."

"Wow. So there's no logical explanation for why your mom is the way you say she is?"

Melanie stood up and walked away from him to look out the window in her living room. "No explanation. That's why I'm so adamant in getting to her whenever she calls me. I'm the only one that can calm her down, and I honestly don't know what she will do to herself if I'm not there." Melanie held herself.

"Have you taken her to see a doctor about it yet?"

"I did and they said it was nothing physical with her, it's all psychological. They said it's something that is so emotional that only she can deal with, but she won't open up. She has scratched herself badly and cut herself at times. That's why I definitely had to have a job where I have the flexibility of checking in on her as needed and the support of my family and friends to do so."

"Cut herself? That's serious, Melanie. Maybe you should admit her somewhere for around the clock care."

"No. I would never put my mother away. She only cut herself a few times and they were superficial cuts. She hasn't done that in years, though."

Andrew walked over to her and rubbed her back as she stared out of the window. "Okay. I'm sorry for even suggesting that." He pulled her closer to him. "So, what do you do for her when you're there?"

"Nothing much, just be there. She just holds me real tight and says that she's sorry. When I ask her what she's sorry for, she never answers. She just squeezes me tighter and continues to say that she's sorry, over and over."

"Wow." Andrew rubbed his face in sheer disbelief. "Why have you never told me about this before?"

"I didn't want to scare you off."

"You can't scare me off. This information only makes me understand you and your situation better. Had I known sooner, maybe I wouldn't have hounded you so much to meet her." He looked into her eyes. He felt sorry for her. She was carrying around her mother's baggage. "Come here." He pulled her into him and held her as tight as he could.

"So, does this mean us getting married is out of the question?" She put her finger up to her chin. "Even though we can't get married just yet anyway because I have to help Karen plan her wedding."

Andrew's eyebrows raised. "Karen is getting married? To who?"

"Ugh, Dennis." Melanie snarled.

"Wow."

"I know, right? But I don't want to talk about them now. Let's get back to us," Melanie demanded.

"I want to marry you, Melanie, but I want us to know each other inside and out before we say 'I do'. And to me, that includes me meeting all of your family."

Melanie looked up at him. "I mean, you can meet my dad, my aunts and uncle, just not my mom, yet."

"Well since your mother is such a big part of your life, I have to meet her, too. Maybe things will be different between her and me when we meet. Maybe she recognized he wasn't the one for you and went ham about that." Andrew laughed.

"I'm just so leery about you all meeting. I don't ever want to relive another day like that again. On a lighter note, I've met your family. They're great and I think we all get along well." Melanie smiled.

"Yeah, you've met my adoptive family, but I still feel some kind of way because I don't know my biological parents and can't introduce you to them.

Like I said before, I love my parents that raised me, but I feel like an unfinished puzzle. Do I have any brothers or sisters out there I don't know about? Nieces? Nephews?"

"I can only imagine how it feels not to know the ones who gave you life, but remember you have a beautiful family that helped to mold you into the man that you are. The fine man that you are." She caressed his cheek. "You ready for dessert?"

"Oh, I've been ready." He scooped her up and took her into her bedroom where he was surprised to find candles already lit and old school R&B playing softly. He looked at her incredulously. "Melanie, are you sure you're ready for this?"

"Yes, I've been ready. Tonight's the night that you make me a woman." She laughed, singing the old-school song by Betty Wright.

Melanie sashayed ahead of him across the room and turned up the volume on her radio. She had a wrap dress on and swayed as she undressed herself.

He walked over to her, trying to grab her, but she pushed him back onto the bed. He laid back on his elbows and watched her as she began a striptease.

She undid her dress.

He stared at her smooth body laden in a leopard print matching bra and panty set. *Damn!* He bit his bottom lip.

She inched her way to him and climbed on top of him and he moaned as she grinded on him. He reached up to grab her neck and moistened it with his tongue.

She pushed his shoulders back down and begin kissing on his neck.

Her phone rang. It was her mother's ringtone.

They both knew she had to take the call.

She rolled over and rushed to her dresser to grab the phone. "Yes, Mom...I'm on my way...Okay."

He looked at her with pleading eyes.

"Andrew, you know I have to go. You're more than welcome to stay. I can't say I'll be back tonight. Nine times out of ten, I won't be, but again, you're more than welcome to stay here. Otherwise, I'll have to catch you tomorrow." She pouted. "Goodnight." She draped her dress back around her body, gave him a quick peck on the lips, and dotted out of her condo.

***

Kyle and his teammates were heading from the locker room to the main floor just before the game started. He could believe they were in the eastern conference finals, but he couldn't believe the text he got from Andrew telling him that Karen was getting married. "Karen is getting married." He found himself saying it out loud as he dribbled the ball.

He tried dating Veronica for a while, but he had to be honest with her and himself; he didn't care about her in a significant way. His heart still belonged to Karen, so he cut it off with Veronica.

He was single and Karen was getting married. That reality played over in his head.

"Kyle, come on, man. Get your head in the game. It's tip-off time. You know what you have to do," the point guard said.

"Yeah, man. I got this."

Kyle didn't win the tip-off and the Toronto Raptors took possession of the ball. However they didn't score from it.

Stacey King and Karen sat on the sideline commenting about the various plays and players, as usual.

Every time Karen looked up, she managed to lock eyes with Dennis across the court. He made funny faces and texted her, even though she wasn't able to respond. He had a show that only taped once a week, so he was able to travel to the various states the Bulls played in to be with Karen and keep tabs on her, and Kyle. He stayed in the hotel room with her whenever he traveled to be with her. He was territorial. He pretty much followed her around like a lost puppy searching for a new home. That fit his plan perfectly.

Kyle couldn't seem to keep his head in the game. Every time the ball was passed to him, he managed to commit a turnover or miss shots he normally made without thinking. The only thing that kept ringing in his head was that Karen was going to marry Dennis. Granted, it had been months since they were together, but he would never discount the times they spent together. It was like none other for him. It didn't compare to anything he had with any other woman. Gabrielle was the only person that seemed to make him happy over the past months without Karen. Her and playing for the Bulls.

It was game six of the NBA Eastern Conference Finals and he knew he needed to focus if his team was going to come out of the east to compete for the national championship. They played through two quarters.

It was half time and the players were on the court warming up for the second half. Kyle tried to get Karen's attention while he was on the floor, but he couldn't seem to pull her attention away from Dennis.

Dennis recognized Kyle trying to get Karen's attention. Between him texting her and mouthing comments to her, he made texts to make sure his plan was still in effect.

The third quarter ended with the Bulls being down by ten. They managed to go on a run in the fourth quarter and get within five points.

Kyle sat out most of the second and third quarters because of his turnovers. The coaches recognized he just couldn't get it together; however, many of the Bulls were in foul trouble and the head coach had no choice but to put Kyle back in.

There were thirty seconds left on the clock in the fourth quarter and the Bulls were down by three. Coach Thibbs had drawn up a play that if the Bulls didn't commit any fouls with the Raptors, they'd be able to get back down to the other end and score three points to tie the game and send them into overtime. The Bulls didn't execute the play the way they should have, but they hustled and scored a two-point field goal to fall within one.

There was now fifteen seconds left on the clock. The Raptors inbounded the ball and tried to shoot a three-pointer to secure the win, but missed and the Bulls were able to get the quick rebound.

The Bulls' point guard ran down the court but was immediately double-teamed. There was no one open to pass the ball to but Kyle.

Kyle was looking off to the side at Karen. She was so beautiful to him. He looked at Dennis across the court blowing kisses at Karen. He hated Dennis.

"Kyle."

Kyle looked up to see the ball coming at him. He reached out and barely caught the ball. He was trying to get his bearings, but the Raptors point guard was quick on his feet. He stole the ball from Kyle, made a fast break running down to the other end, and dunked the ball clenching the Raptors win.

There would automatically be a game seven. The series was going back to Chicago.

Kyle walked back to the locker room with his head down. He stayed away from his teammates believing they were upset with him because he committed such a rookie turnover. He quickly showered, dressed, and left.

He made it to the car where his driver was waiting for him, but before he could get in, he was accosted by Porsha and Unique. They were different this time. Porsha had already given birth and Unique seemed as if she was due any day.

"What's the matter, Kyle? Can't win a game?" Porsha said, rocking the crying newborn.

"Don't worry, girl. He's still paid. It's okay, Kyle. You need me to cheer you up?" Unique licked her lips and twirled her hair.

He looked at them contemptuously. He didn't bother to respond to what they were saying. "Excuse me, ladies." He squeezed past them.

"Unh, unh. Where you going? Don't you want to meet your other daughter?" Porsha moved towards him.

"Kyle Jr. ain't made his arrival yet, but he'll be here any day now." Unique rubbed her belly.

Kyle gave them a piercing look.

Unique backed up some shielding her belly, but Porsha knew they had to keep egging him on. "Kyle, when can we take the paternity test? You've been busy with these games, but we need to get the results back so that you could start running me my money."

He looked back at them. "Monday morning. I've been ready to take the test. You all have been dodging my lawyer."

"What? No, they have been saying that you've been dodging us."

"Nope. The last game of this series is on Sunday night, so I'll be free Monday morning to get this over with. I'll have my lawyers set up the appointment and forward the location of the doctor's office and time to your lawyers."

Porsha and Unique's eyes darted back and forth between one another.

Unique said, "Give me your cell number and we'll call you. We don't need those lawyers for this. They cost too much anyway."

"Nope. I'll have Andrew call your lawyers with the details." He managed to push past the women and get into the car. The driver sped off.

Porsha looked at Unique. "Girl, he's actually willing to take the test. What are we going to do now?"

.

24

Karen couldn't believe that Kyle committed such a rookie turnover, sending the Bulls to a game seven.

Today, she should have been able to just enjoy picking out a wedding dress and a maid of honor dress for Melanie, but that feat wouldn't be as glorious as she wanted it to be. She would have to speed through her bridal appointment to make sure that she was done in time to cover the game that evening.

She and Melanie went to a few wedding boutiques around town. They were well pleased with the last one they visited. The dresses they wanted were in stock and would be cleaned, tailored, and ready by the soon approaching wedding date.

Karen settled on a simple yet elegant off-white sweetheart neckline trumpet style dress that hugged her in all the right places. She allowed Melanie to pick the dress and color she wanted. Melanie chose a midnight blue chiffon gown. The color consciously mirrored her feelings about the pending nuptials.

Later on that evening, Karen and Stacey reported the game as usual. They definitely enjoyed and fed off the energy of the Chicago Bulls crowd. She was grateful and honored that her hometown team was aggressive, especially on defense and strong on offense. They beat the Raptors by twenty points to win the Eastern Conference Finals. They were headed to the national finals against the Golden State Warriors starting the next week.

Since the series they were in went to seven games, she would literally only have but a couple of free days to flesh out the rest of the details for her wedding before the championship series started.

Thank God for speech recognition software. Because of it, she was able to talk out the articles she had for upcoming deadlines, leaving her hands free to complete other tasks, like driving or surfing the web for wedding favors for her guests. Her long-term assistant knew exactly how to edit the articles to her liking. She emailed them to her assistant the minute she said the last words for each one.

Dennis was out of town on assignment, leaving her to plan the rest of the wedding on her own, but that was okay with her because she knew she could count on Melanie to help her.

Karen had just taken a quart of ice cream out the freezer and was putting scoops into a bowl when her door flung open. It's was Melanie's usual grand entrance.

"Oh, I see that you're about to spend some quality time with your best friend." Melanie laughed, watching Karen scoop the ice cream.

"Whatever. Baskin Robbins has always been there for me." Karen playfully rolled her eyes.

"So are you saying that I haven't been there for you?" Melanie bucked her eyes and snapped her neck.

Karen laughed. "No. I'm not saying that. Of course, you have always been here. We just don't want to ignore the third friend in this relationship... ice cream." She laughed again and licked the spoon.

"You are so silly. Well, I guess we can add Dennis Michaels to that list now." Melanie frowned.

"Yes, we can. I see you're still not sold on him. You rolled your eyes at the mention of his name." Karen put the spoon down.

Melanie sat down at the stool across from Karen. "Karen, talk to me. I mean really talk to me. Are you sure that you're ready to get married? Let alone get married to Dennis?"

"Yes. I know that I'm ready to get married. You know for a fact that it has been a sincere desire of mine to have the kind of marriage, the kind of love that my parents had." Her eyes misted. "I'm more than ready to get married."

"There's nothing wrong with wanting to get married or getting married. The issue is with *who* you marry and *why* you marry him."

"And what's wrong with me marrying Dennis?" Karen put her hands on her hips.

"Because it's Dennis, not Kyle." Melanie held her hands up as if to say, 'You should already know that.'

"Why do you always manage to bring Kyle Irving into our conversation? That was so last year. I enjoyed the time that I spent with him." Karen smiled. "And then it was over." She snarled. "Clearly I have moved on." She waved her left hand to show off the exquisite diamond on her ring finger.

"I don't care about that ring on your finger. I'm more concerned with what's in your heart. Can you honestly tell me that you are completely over Kyle Irving?"

Karen was silent.

"Why the rush? You went right from being with Kyle to being with Dennis, and then saying 'yes' so soon to marrying him."

"Yes, Melanie. Dennis and I are getting married soon and not too long into our relationship, and there's nothing wrong with that."

Melanie huffed loudly expressing her disdain.

"First off, there is no set timeline for love, for weddings, for babies. Yes, couples normally wait a year after getting engaged before they get married, but that's because they have to save money for the ceremony and wait for the venue they want to be available. Well, Dennis and I aren't the average couple. We don't have to save money to pay for the wedding, and yes our semi-celebrity status helped us to get a venue that otherwise may not have been available for another year. So we don't have to wait a year, and I don't see anything wrong with that." Karen cocked her head matter-of-factly at Melanie as if saying, "That's that."

Melanie laughed. "You still haven't answered my question."

"What question?"

"Are you really over Kyle?"

"For the millionth time, yes, I am over Kyle." Karen's breathing sped up and she crossed her arms at her chest. "That was so long ago and a short encounter might I add." She pointed at Melanie.

Melanie shook her head and stopped thumbing through the bridal magazine. She squinted her eyes and leaned towards Karen. "I don't care how short your time was with him, need I remind you about your time spent with him in St. Lucia. You spent every waking moment of that week with him. And you would only give a man that much of your time if your feelings were genuine and deep for him."

Karen averted eye contact with Melanie as she scarfed down her ice cream.

"As much as you try to downplay what you had with him, your constant running away from the subject and him further proves my point of how much in love you were, *are*, with him. No other man has ever had that kind of impact on you. So yes, I find it hard to believe that you are fully over Kyle, let alone 'in love' with Dennis to marry him."

Karen leaned back against the kitchen countertop eating her ice cream and meditating on what Melanie had said. She finally decided to speak. "I hear you and I see your air quotes. Kyle was my brief then, but Dennis is my now and my future. I wish you would understand that and respect my decision to marry Kyle, I mean Dennis." Karen turned her back towards Melanie. She rubbed her forehead. She couldn't believe she slipped at the tongue like that.

Melanie laughed. "See, it's things like that that confirms you're not over Kyle. He still gets under your skin at the games and you're very snide with him when you have to interact with him even though it's a part of your job. I've seen some of those interviews you've done with him this season. You barely make eye contact with him and you're very curt with him. A woman only acts that way with a man when she still has feelings for him. Otherwise, you would stand confident as you speak to him because you know he still doesn't have a hold on your heart."

Karen picked at invisible lint on her shirt.

"That's okay. Ignore me if you want to. You're only pretending to do so because you know I'm right. You're just too afraid to admit it to me, but most importantly, to yourself. Did you ever figure out the difference between loving someone versus being in love with them?"

"Yes, I've been told you I knew the difference."

"Well, what's the difference then?" Melanie sat back in the stool and crossed her arms to listen carefully to Karen.

Karen cleared her throat. She put her ice cream down. "You can and should love everyone. You respect who they are regardless of what they may have done, but when you're in love with someone, a man in my case, your souls connect on a level unlike a connection with anyone else. It's unconditional. It goes beyond borders. Without limits. You trust them with your life, and would give yours for theirs." Karen was happy with her response. She smiled.

"So, do you just love Dennis or are you in love with him?"

"I love Dennis." Karen paused, turning her back towards Melanie. "And I don't want to talk about this anymore. Okay, let's get back to planning this wedding, this spectacular wedding of me marrying Dennis, the man that I love." Karen grabbed the quart of ice cream and headed to her dining table.

"Mmph. Don't you think that you've had enough ice cream already? I know I've had enough bologna for the day." Melanie bore a playful grin on her face.

Karen waved her hand dismissively at Melanie.

They sat down and detailed how the wedding ceremony would flow. Seeing as though Melanie was her closest and really her only friend, the wedding party would be small.

Karen was somewhat of a private person, so there wouldn't be that many people in attendance for the wedding, which was two weeks away. Invitations had already been sent out to the guests. She had a wedding coordinator, but she still wanted to relish in planning her own wedding.

Karen and Melanie discussed as much of what had not already been talked about with the wedding planner and she enjoyed the rest of the evening with her best friend pigging out on junk food and watching movies. She knew tying the knot would change nights like that. Being married would require giving more time to Dennis than what she was already giving him and leaving even less room to spend with Melanie.

25

Melanie stood in her knee-length, midnight blue, chiffon dress in the hallway of the church ready to march in before Karen. The length of the dress matched her feelings about the ceremony and Karen's wedding. She hoped the ceremony would be short and sadly, she hoped their marriage wouldn't last long either.

She dismissed her thoughts of Karen and Dennis when her mom, Marie, came out of the sanctuary. Melanie loved her mother dearly but was hesitant to bring her to the wedding because she knew Andrew wanted to attend as her date. When Karen insisted that her mother be there, she begged Andrew at the last minute not to come because she still wasn't ready for him to meet her mom. He saw the desperation in her eyes and agreed not to come.

"Mom, you look so beautiful." She pulled Marie towards her and kissed her cheek.

Marie gave Melanie a curt smile. "Where's the restroom?" she whispered.

"That way." Melanie pointed to her right. "Hurry up and get back before the ceremony starts."

"Okay, sweetie." Marie rushed off.

Melanie smelled the intoxicating sporty scent of Andrew's cologne before she saw him. But it couldn't be him, he agreed not to come.

He came up to her and kissed her on her cheek. "You look angelic."

"Thank you." She narrowed her eyes in on him. "Why are you here?"

"I wanted to come and support Karen." He laughed.

"Whatever. We both know why you're here, but I'm begging you not to say anything to me or my mother when you see us together."

Andrew's shoulders slumped. "Okay."

"Thanks. Now hurry up and go get a seat before this angel walks down the aisle." She winked.

Andrew took his time pulling away from Melanie as he mouthed naughty things to her.

Melanie was flirting back with him and didn't notice her mom's closeness to her until she felt her mother's hand on her back and heard her say something. Nervous, she yelled, "Mom. What are you doing?" She dropped her bouquet.

"Let me get that for you, babe." Andrew stooped down to get the fallen flowers.

"I'm just tucking in the tag on your dress. But why did that man call you babe?" Marie's voice shook.

Andrew stalled getting up from the floor. He had heard that voice before. The last time he heard it with that same shakiness in it was when he was four years old. It was the voice of the woman who left him when he was a little boy. Shoulders tense and temples throbbing, he slowly stood up straight and held his breath as he looked past Melanie into Marie's eyes. It was those same eyes that Melanie had that always made him feel like he knew her. His stomach churned.

Is that the chemistry he had with Melanie?

Melanie could tell that something was wrong with Andrew from the horrid look on his face. "What's wrong?"

Marie forgot how to breathe staring at Andrew. She dropped her purse to her side. Her hands shook. Her lips trembled. "Andrew? Andrew, is that you?"

Melanie turned quickly to look at her mom. "How did you know his name?"

Andrew walked closer until he almost stood in between them.

Marie moved back.

Melanie's eyebrows raised as her eyes widened. "Can someone please explain to me what's going on? Andrew, why are you acting like that? Mom, are you okay? Do you need to step outside for a second?"

"Baby, I'm sorry. I'm so sorry." Marie put her shaky hands up to her quivering lips. Her tears flowed. "Baby, I'm so sorry."

"Mom you always tell me you're sorry, but you never tell me what you're sorry for. Everything is fine. You didn't do anything wrong to me, if that's what you think. Everything is okay."

Marie continued mumbling. "I'm so sorry, baby. I'm so sorry, baby." She stared at Andrew, but Melanie was oblivious to that.

"Ma, what are you sorry about?"

"I think she's talking to me." Andrew touched Melanie's shoulder as he moved past her to draw closer to Marie.

Melanie bucked her eyes at Andrew. "What are you talking about?"

He took deep, slow breaths. "She's talking to me."

"Why would she be telling you she's sorry? Why would she be calling you baby? She doesn't even know you." Melanie's forehead creased as she placed her hands on her hips.

Marie reached her hand out to Andrew, but pulled it back. She placed both of her hands on her temples and shook her head from side to side. "I'm so sorry. I'm so sorry. I'm so sorry. I'm so sorry." She paused for what seemed like an eternity to Andrew and Melanie. "If I could turn back the hands of time, I never would have gave you up. I'm so sorry. I just couldn't continue to look at you after what he did to me. You looked just like him."

Melanie was utterly confused. "Mom, what are you talking about?"

"Ma," Andrew called out.

She remained silent, allowing the tears to flow down her face without interruption.

"Mom?" Andrew whispered, drawing even closer to Marie.

"Yes," Marie uttered slowly and lifted her head gradually until she timidly looked him directly in his eyes.

Eyebrows raised high and nostrils flared. Melanie looked between the both of them.

"Andrew, did you just call my mother Mom?"

He said nothing.

She looked to Marie. "Ma, did you just answer him when he called you Mom?"

Marie finally turned her attention to Melanie. She took a deep breath before she spoke, trying to even her breathing. "Melanie, I'm so sorry I never told you."

Melanie moved past Andrew and stood in front of Marie. "Never told me what?"

Marie sighed deeply. "I was raped and I got pregnant. I had Andrew. I tried my best to love him, but I just couldn't. He looked so much like..." Marie's eyes welled up with more tears and the salty water spilled down her face. "I, I couldn't stomach seeing him anymore...I had to give him away." She reached out towards Andrew but drew her hand back. "I couldn't give him the love that he needed..." Marie hung her head.

Melanie's mouth dropped open. Her temples pounded, and she could hear her heart beat in her ears. "I'm sorry, something must be wrong with my ears." She clicked her tongue. She drew in a deep breath, closed her mouth, held her nostrils closed, and tried to push air through her ears hoping to clear her hearing.

Marie looked up at Melanie. "You heard me right. Andrew is the son I had and gave away before I had you." She exhaled loudly.

Melanie shook her head rapidly from side to side before she said, "So you're telling me that Andrew," she pointed towards him, "the man that I love, the man that I've spent months with, is your son? My brother?"

Melanie stuck her neck out and turned her head so that her mom would speak directly into her ear. She wanted her ear to catch every syllable her mother said this time.

Marie's pupils dilated. Her mouth dropped open. "What do you mean the man you've loved for months? I didn't know that you were dating him. You never told me you were dating anyone for that matter." Marie covered her mouth.

"I never could, Mom." Melanie threw the bouquet down this time and let her long arms slap her thighs in frustration. "You always went crazy at the mention of me having a boyfriend. You went berserk the last time I brought one home for you to meet. I was too scared to ever bring someone to you."

"Baby, I'm so sorry. I was messed up and I guess I messed you up..." Marie hugged herself. She looked into Andrew's eyes but directed her speech at Melanie. "Seeing Andrew today, it just did something to me. It woke me up out of this stupor I've been in for so long."

Melanie shook her head. "Ahhhhhh. I can't. I can't deal with this right now." Her eyebrows furrowed. Her nose scrunched. "Andrew, the man that I'm in love with is my brother?" She gripped her stomach and mouth trying to calm her queasiness.

Andrew was just as shocked as Melanie, but he had to admit that he was happy to finally meet the woman that gave him life. To reconnect with the woman that had those eyes that he couldn't get out of his head was amazingly weird to him. He realized the connection he had with Melanie wasn't because he loved her and was attracted to her, but because she was his sister with the same eyes as his mother; the first woman he ever loved even though she never seemed to love him back.

Melanie tried to speak, but the queasiness in her stomach overtook her. She ran to the bathroom holding her stomach and mouth.

Having heard the entire conversation between Melanie, Marie, and Andrew, Karen stood by in complete disbelief. It was her wedding day. She would already have to cut her time short with her soon-to-be-husband to go and broadcast the game later on that night, and on top of that, she just witnessed her best friend find out that her boyfriend was really her brother. She thought those things only happened in the movies.

She came out of her daze and grabbed her dress as best as she could and ran to the bathroom. "Melanie? Where are you? Melanie?"

The toilet flushed and Melanie finally came out of a stall. She went to the faucet and rinsed her mouth out and patted cold water on her face.

"Stop splashing that water on your face, you'll ruin your makeup." Karen stood next to Melanie and rubbed her back.

"Who cares about makeup at a time like this?"

"You're right. I'm sorry. Are you okay, sweetie?"

Melanie braced her hands on the sink and stared into the mirror. Her eyes were bloodshot red. Her breathing was uneven. "No. I'm not okay. I can't believe this, Karen. I can't believe that the man that I love or used to love is my brother. I kissed my brother." Melanie ran back into the stall to throw up.

Karen followed Melanie. She bent down to make sure that Melanie's hair was out of the way as Melanie relieved herself.

"Did you..." Karen was hesitant to finish her question.

"No." Melanie stood up and wiped her mouth then flushed the toilet. She walked past Karen plastered against the stall wall. "Thank God I didn't go that far with him." Melanie turned to face Karen. She gripped her shoulders. "Oh my God, Karen. I've been in love with my brother all of this time."

"I know this is all surreal right now, but Melanie, you had no clue that you had a brother, let alone that Andrew was your brother. So, technically it's not your fault."

"I know that in the back of my head, but to know that he's my brother and he's had his tongue down my throat," Melanie fought the urge to throw up again, "I can't deal with it."

"Well, honey. Do you still want to walk down the aisle? Because I totally understand if you don't want to," Karen asked, concerned for her friend's state of mind.

"Karen, I'm so sorry. I'm carrying on frantic and all like my mother." She shook her head and laughed. "This is your day, and I want to be here for you, just as much and you've been there for me throughout my life. This is just something that I'll have to deal with after you get hitched." Melanie shook her shoulders as if she was trying to shake off every moment of kissing Andrew. "I'm sorry for delaying the wedding from starting, but let's get back out there and get you married, if that's what you really want to do."

"Why would you ask that?"

"It just came to me, but isn't it strange that this happened right before your wedding. You sure it's not a sign?"

"It wasn't for me, it was a sign to you. I'm sure that I want to marry Kyle, I mean Dennis."

Melanie tried to speak, but Karen held her hands up in protest. "Don't you say a word." Karen walked out first and Melanie threw up one last time before following suit.

***

Andrew and Marie tried to speak to Melanie, but she silenced them with her finger. "We'll talk about this later. Right now, my best friend is getting married and this moment is about her."

They heard the firmness in her voice and knew it was best not to press the issue.

Andrew extended his arm out to Marie. "May I escort you to your seat?"

Marie exhaled slowly. "Yes." She smiled. Marie wiped a tear from her eye, interlaced her elbow with his, and they walked into the sanctuary together and sat next to each other near the front of the church.

***

The wedding planner signaled the musicians to start the music. The door was opened and Melanie walked through it.

Her feet were heavy as she trudged her way down the aisle while the speakers blared "You" by Jesse Powell. She made eye contact with her mother and Andrew but quickly turned away. She tried to keep her tears at bay and her stomach from turning, listening to the words of the song,

The way you walk, the way you talk
The way you say my name and smile
The way you move me, the way you soothe me
The way you speak softly through the night
Every morning you rise and open your eyes
I just wanna be there with you baby
I just wanna be yours from this day forth...

Earlier that day, she felt every one of those sentiments for Andrew, but now that she knew he was her brother, she wished her bouquet was a brick that she could use to shatter the speakers, just like her world had been shattered.

She managed to make it to the lit arch at the front of the church where she would stand until the ceremony was over.

The flower girls came in next. They were Marge's granddaughters. Their off white, fluffy, tulle dresses swayed as they sped down the aisle throwing white rose pedals as their spiraled ponytails and white ribbons flopped on their heads.

Dennis' nephew, a handsome little snaggletooth ring bearer, pranced down the aisle right after them. He dropped the pillow several times while people in the crowd cheered him on and chatted about how adorable he was.

He stopped at Dennis. "Here, lil' man. Stand here." It took Dennis some doing, but he was able to get the ring bearer to stand still long enough so that the ceremony could continue.

Dennis stood there with his hands behind his back smiling as he heard the music that would cue Karen to walk down the aisle. He requested that she walk down the aisle to "All My Life" by the R&B duo K-Ci and Jo-Jo. He really believed that she was the one that he had wanted all of his life, and he did what he thought he had to do to get and keep her.

Karen took deep breaths as she stood in front of the door waiting for her signal to enter. She wished dearly that her father could be there to share the coveted moment with her, but since he wasn't, she had no choice but to walk the aisle alone as the center of attention.

Her short hair was feathered to one side so that the birdcage hat with a lace veil off to the left side of her face would fit perfectly on top of her head.

With her dress hugging her in all of the right places, she knew that Dennis would be pleased with what he saw.

The doors opened and Karen appeared. She looked like an angel. There was even a stream of light from the windows behind her that cast an ethereal glow on her natural beauty.

"Karen, go," the wedding coordinator whispered loudly, unseen by those inside the sanctuary.

She took a deep breath and walked gracefully as she swayed down the aisle. She worked hard to erase the doubts racing through her head as she glided closer to Dennis. His eyes were just as glossy as hers were, which let her know that he was trying to fight back tears, too.

She hoped his were not tears of doubt though.

***

Kyle didn't know if he should leave well enough alone or if he should use the information he found out to expose the truth. After all, he felt that she should know before she made such a life altering decision.

That night was game seven of the NBA Finals and he was a part of the starting lineup. He knew he needed to be at the stadium in an hour for warm-ups and stretching. That left him with no time to get across town and back without possibly getting fined by the team's management and berated by the coach. But his mind was made up and his heart was leading him. He would take the risk.

He put on his warm-up gear and headed out the door to his car and across town.

Kyle's nerves danced as he drove. He imagined someone doing somersaults in his stomach. He was nervous about the information that he had to share, which affected both him and her; but also, the traffic he was stuck in. Apparently, everyone was making their way to the United Center for the game and the slow moving bumper to bumper cars shortened the time frame he mapped out for his impromptu plan. He managed to carefully weave in and out of the traffic and finally made it to the church. He jumped out of the car and doubled up the stairs. His sweaty hand gripped the doorknob, but he let it slip through his grip. He was having second thoughts. *Are you seriously about to do this, dude?* He put caution to the wind and pulled the door open. He stepped into the hallway of the church with its massive ceilings. His 6'5" frame felt small.

His thoughts fell back in line with his task at hand. He knew he needed to tell her even if she didn't want to hear it. He felt she still deserved to know the truth.

He could hear the preacher. "Marriage is a covenant between you, you, and God. On this day, you two establish that you are forever bound to one another, not with chains as in oppression or jail, but with love. You are to uphold one another, protect one another, cover one another, remain truthful to one another…"

Kyle laughed to himself thinking the preacher's words didn't describe Karen and Dennis in the least bit. Thanks to the speakers in the hallway, Kyle knew it was at the point of the ceremony where the bride and groom had to recite their vows to one another.

He nodded his head at a janitor as he walked past.

"I, Karen Charice Roberts, take you, Dennis Steven Michaels, to be my husband, my partner in life, and my one true love."

Kyle remained in the hallway laughing and mumbling to himself. "One true love? Yeah right." His thoughts refocused to what was being said over the speakers.

"I, I will cherish our union and love you more each day than I did the day before. I will trust you and respect you, laugh with you and cry with you, loving you faithfully through good times and bad, regardless of the obstacles we may face together. I give you my hand, my, my…"

Kyle mumbled again, "You can't say it because it's not true." He shook his head in frustration.

He tuned back in to see if Karen would lie.

"…my heart…" She did. She whispered the words the rest of the way. "…and my love." There was a long pause before she spoke again. "From this day forward for as long as we both shall live."

He heard her sniffling. His ears were hot and his nostrils flared. He knew that the minister had already asked if there was someone there to object. Since he missed that cue, he wondered if that was a sign that he should leave and head to the stadium, but he heard gum smacking behind him and there was a tap on his shoulder. He looked at them. "I thought you all wouldn't come."

"You threatened us. We had no choice," Unique said, laughing.

"Besides, we don't like him anyway. He's a jerk," Porsha chimed in, popping her gum.

"Good, we're on the same page. Let's go in then." Kyle perked up. He hoped that Karen would forgive and thank him for interrupting her special day. He stopped in front of the doors to the sanctuary. He took a deep breath before he snatched open the heavy, tall doors bringing everyone's attention to him.

Karen gasped. She looked at Kyle then at Dennis.

Dennis's eyebrows raised as he looked at who was behind Kyle. He dashed past Karen and darted into the aisle.

Kyle confidently walked up the aisle with Unique and Porsha following closely behind him.

The two men met one another half-way down the aisle.

Dennis came eye to eye with Kyle. "What are you doing here?" He balled his fists up and clenched his jaws.

"I need to speak to Karen. Get out of the way."

"No, you will not speak to my wife. Security." Dennis looked around hoping that there was someone there to remove Kyle, but security wasn't hired for the wedding. The security guard on duty for the church was a portly old man barely able to walk down the aisle straight, let alone remove Kyle.

Dennis knew his scrawny best man was no match for Kyle.

Everyone in the congregation seemed to hold their breaths waiting to see what would happen next. The only sounds heard in the church as Dennis scanned the sanctuary looking for someone to come to his aid was the gum popping of Porsha.

Karen finally came out of her state of shock and stomped down the aisle to where Kyle and Dennis stood. She stepped in between them sensing they were about to go head to head.

"Kyle. What are you doing here?" She tried to sound upset, but the smell of his cologne and her closeness to him weakened her.

"Karen, there's something I need to tell you." Kyle stared into her eyes.

"Shut up. Stop talking to my wife." Dennis shouted in fury at Kyle.

"You didn't say I do yet. She's not your wife."

Dennis tried to move Karen out of the way, but she didn't budge.

"Kyle, what are you doing here? And why did you bring them in here?" She pointed to the women behind him. Karen's nostrils flared and her eyes narrowed in on him.

"Dennis can tell you better than I can." Kyle grimaced.

Karen bucked her head in bewilderment at Kyle, but turned to face Dennis. She tilted her head, her eyebrows raised. The fierce look in her eyes demanded him to answer her.

"Ignore him, Karen. He's just upset that I got you and he didn't." Dennis looked over Karen's head. "Just go back to wherever you came from."

Kyle didn't flinch.

"I gave you the chance to tell her, but you didn't." Kyle grabbed Karen by the shoulders and made her face him.

The touch between them was electrifying.

He looked into her eyes. "Karen, Dennis is not the man you think he is."

"What are you talking about?" Karen said.

Dennis leaned over and whispered in Karen's ear.

Kyle was annoyed with the remarks he overheard from Dennis. "Yes, I have a beautiful daughter with Mercedes." He looked deeper into Karen's eyes. "I'm sorry that you didn't know that in the beginning when we first fell in—"

She waved her hand dismissively to stop Kyle from speaking any further. "Kyle, I know that's not what you came here for." Karen's eyes watered. "And besides, that was so long ago. I'm over that. I'm over you. I'm over your other baby mommas, too."

"See, girl, we tried to come up in here to save her, and see how funky she's acting?" Porsha snapped.

"Girl, can't you see that's just her hurt and pride talking? She ain't got real beef with us," Unique said.

"You know what? You right. I see it all in her eyes." Porsha stepped out from behind Kyle to get a better look at Karen. "Mmhh, hmmm. Girl, you shole right."

"Will you please just leave now?" Karen choked on her words staring at Kyle.

"Karen, I didn't come here to hurt you. I came here to set the record straight. I only have one child and that's Gabrielle. These other two women—"

"Shut up, man. Get out of here." Dennis reached past Karen and pushed Kyle.

Kyle took a deep breath. His eyes narrowed in on Dennis. "You better be glad Karen is standing here or else…"

"Or else what?" Dennis puffed his chest out seeing that his best man had come and stood next to him. He felt that the two of them combined had a better chance of taking Kyle down than they each had alone.

Andrew made his way over to the heated crowd and stood near Kyle. He'd battle others with his best friend if he need be, but just meeting the woman he'd longed to know for so long left him speechless as he stood near Kyle.

"Don't test me." The bass in Kyle's voice bellowed throughout the church. "You're just lucky that Karen is in between us." He looked down at Karen. "I would never do anything to intentionally hurt you."

It was all too much for Karen. The sincerity in his voice, memories of their time in St. Lucia where Kyle had branded himself in her heart and their moments spent together after that played in her mind. She was so confused. "You would never do anything to intentionally hurt me, but you burst into my wedding and ruin this day for me. And you still haven't told me exactly why you're here. But you say you'd never do anything to intentionally hurt me?" She poked him in his chest.

Kyle ignored the shove Karen gave him. He looked down in her eyes, they danced with confusion, hurt, and love.

"Karen, like I said, Gabrielle is my only child." He turned to point at Unique and Porsha. "These two women that have been claiming that I'm the father of their children have been lying because this fool right here paid them off." He pointed at Dennis and shook his head.

Dennis tried to go around Karen to get to Kyle, but Karen stopped him.

"Man, stop lying. I did no such thing." Dennis pointed at Kyle.

"Kyle, what are you talking about?" Karen's arm remained up, holding back Dennis as she stared into Kyle's eyes.

"I have proof that Dennis paid both of them all of this time to say that I fathered their children. He wanted you to not want me anymore."

"Shut up, man." Dennis charged at Kyle, but Karen turned towards him and halted his steps.

"Shut up, Dennis." Karen faced him. She turned back to Kyle. "Why should I believe you? What proof do you have?"

"Well, they're here as proof, but I had my lawyer do some digging into the matter and come to find out that they had large sums of money being deposited into their accounts monthly."

Karen's eyebrows raised.

Kyle knew he was drawing Karen in so he continued talking. "And when they traced the source of the money, it went back to this creep, Dennis." Kyle laughed. "He wasn't even smart enough to pay them in cash or to create a dummy account. He was paying them right out of his checking account."

Dennis's nostrils flared. His jaws clenched. He rounded Karen and charged at Kyle trying to shut him up, but Kyle overpowered him and gripped him in a headlock.

Karen threw her bouquet down, staring at Dennis. "Is this the truth?"

His eyes bucked. His mouth was dry. "No, honey. It's not true. Don't believe him."

Porsha came from behind Kyle and stood next to Karen. "Yeah, girl. What Kyle said is true. This loser right here," she smacked her lips and pointed at Dennis, "contacted us and asked us if we wanted to make some money."

"Of course we did," Unique chimed in.

Porsha looked remorseful. "So we went along with it. Shoot, girl, he paid us five thousand dollars a month each, so it was nothing for us to leave Miami and come here to set Kyle up. We were already pregnant."

Karen couldn't believe what she was hearing. The day was getting worse as it went on. She knew she had doubts in the back of her mind about marrying

Dennis, but to have this confirmation was overwhelming for her.

She snapped out of her thoughts. "Dennis, how could you? How could you? Why would you betray me like this?" Karen's lips curved down.

"I didn't betray you, sweetie. I never did anything to hurt you. I've loved you since high school." Dennis reached out to Karen, but she pulled away from him.

"What?" Karen snapped her neck back as her eyes widened.

"You still don't remember me?"

"What are you talking about?" Karen was confused.

"Karen, we went to high school together."

"No, we didn't."

"Yes, we did, Karen. I didn't look like how I do now and we never talked, but we did go to high school together." Dennis exhaled loudly.

Karen grabbed her forehead. "But I would've remembered you if I went to high school with you."

Distraught and trying to keep herself from wilting, Melanie moved closer to Karen's side. "You okay?"

Karen looked at Melanie barely holding it together. "I'm okay, Mel." She wished she could help her best friend to make sense of the blow she was just dealt. Melanie's looked flush, but Karen needed to get to the bottom of the catastrophe unfolding in front of her. She refocused her attention on Dennis as he reached into his back pocket and grabbed his wallet. He pulled out a tattered picture of him and handed it to her.

She stared at it. "Who is this?"

"Me."

"This can't be you."

"It is. This was how I looked in high school." Dennis said matter-of-factly.

"But I don't remember you."

"I can see that. I've always remembered you. Loved you. I was scrawny, and I admit I was nerdy back then. I was always getting stuffed into lockers or my head dunked in toilets by the jocks on the football and basketball teams. Well one day, you saw them trying to stuff me in a locker and you came to my rescue. You made them stop."

Karen stood cemented in place with her eyebrows furrowed.

"That was the only time you ever spoke to me or looked me in my eyes, but I knew at that moment that I loved you and I always would. We had classes together over the years, but I could never work up the courage to talk to you. I heard about your parents passing and my heart went out to you because my mom had died the year before. I wanted to be there for you the way you were there for me that day at my locker. I went to the funeral to console you but you were there wrapped in the arms of the captain of the basketball team. I never got my chance with you then, but I vowed that if I ever saw you again I would make you mine."

Karen slowly shook her head in awe.

Dennis became excited thinking about how they met up again. "Don't you see that it was fate that we majored in the same thing and landed at the same network together?"

Karen stepped back from him.

"I could tell that when we first reacquainted at the station that you didn't remember me, but that was okay, I was going to make you love me. The glasses, pimples, braces, and jerry curl is gone and I've filled out well with my muscles. I was making good money and we had the love of sports in common." Dennis was still in Kyle's vice grip of a headlock.

"Why didn't you ever say any of this to me before?" Karen was baffled.

"I planned to after we were married. I thought it was best if I built a friendship with you first and then I would make my move on you, but Kyle messed that up in St. Lucia. So I did what I needed to do to get you once and for all."

Karen's eyebrows scrunched, mirroring the mix of emotions swirling in her head. The veins in her neck throbbed as she elevated on the tip of her toes to be somewhat eye level with him. "I can't believe what I'm hearing. You knew me, but never told me that. You were dishonest in winning me over. Making me feel safe and comfortable with you, when clearly you're conniving and will do anything to get what you want."

"Girl, I might as well tell you. You know your partner Stacey King?" Porsha spoke.

Karen looked bewildered at Porsha. "Yeah."

"Girl, this fool told us he used to poison Stacey so that Stacey would be sick and unable to cover the games with you. He fixed everything so he could be your co-host. Girl, he wanted to keep tabs on you and Kyle. He is too dirty."

Karen's eyes narrowed in on him and her lips formed a snarl. "You really did that to Stacey?"

Dennis struggled to get out of the headlock but refused to answer her.

"You low down dirty... I could never be with someone like you." Karen recoiled away from Dennis.

Dennis was enraged. He muscled himself away from Kyle and pushed Kyle back from him in the chest. "Man, this is all your fault."

Kyle laughed and charged at Dennis, but Karen stepped in front of him.

Her action gave Dennis more gall to continue talking. "If you would've never came to St. Lucia after I had tracked her down, I wouldn't have had to do all of this."

Karen's eyes bulged. She stared at Dennis. "You tracked me down?"

Dennis's eyes softened when he spoke to Karen. "I'm sorry." Dennis rubbed his forehead. "I did some digging to find out the exact hotel you would be at. I wanted to be there with you."

Karen threw her hands up. "What haven't you done?" She tried to walk past him, but he stretched his arms out and blocked the aisle.

"I have always loved you and wanted to be with you." He got down on his knees in front of her. "You know we're meant to be together. Just give me another chance. I love you, Karen."

She laughed and clapped her hands rapidly.

Dennis's eyebrows furrowed.

Her laughter subsided so that she could speak. "Thank you for being you."

"What do you mean?" He remained on his knees.

"Shut up." The veins in her neck throbbed. "I'm glad I found out about the *real* you before I said I do."

She tried to walk off, but Dennis thwarted her attempt yet again.

She growled, staring down at his hand on her wrist.

Kyle moved closer to her.

Her lips were tight and her eyes were beady. "Let go of me."

Dennis didn't want to let go of her, but he heard the venom in her voice and heeded her request.

She laughed at herself before speaking. "I can admit it to myself now. I was never in love with you. I was in love with being married and starting a family. I'm not ashamed of it either because nothing is wrong with that. I just need to wait for the right one to catch me."

Karen brushed past Kyle and ran down the aisle picking up the pace as she got closer to the door. She ran straight out of the building and into the parking lot towards her car. She was breathing heavily by the time she made it there so she leaned across her car to catch her breath.

Melanie ran out soon after Karen, but not before she snatched Karen's purse from the wedding coordinator posted at the door. She made her way to the parking lot and finally caught up with Karen.

They both panted, trying to catch their breaths.

"Karen, are you okay? Are you okay?"

Karen turned around. Tears streamed her face.

"I can't believe that just happened. And in front of everybody. We both had a crazy day, hunh?"

They both shook their heads at one another in agreement but started laughing hysterically.

"I guess we have to laugh to keep from crying," Melanie said.

"Or ripping someone's head off," Karen chimed in.

They buckled over in laughter. It was the best way to release the myriad of emotions running through them.

Kyle slowly walked towards Karen's car. He didn't know what to make of the beautiful woman in the wedding dress slumped over laughing along with her best friend. He cleared his throat as he neared them.

Melanie heard footsteps behind her. She wiped her tears of laughter and turned around.

Karen was still buckled over laughing with her head tucked low.

"Karen, are you okay?" Melanie asked.

"Yeah, I'll be okay."

"Well here's your purse. I'll just be over there if you need me." She pointed to the entrance of the church.

Melanie patted Kyle's arm as she walked past him.

He teetered from his heels to toes as Karen stood up, smoothing out her dress.

"Look, Karen. I'm sorry. I didn't come here to ruin your day or upset you. I just wanted you to know the truth before you said I do to him."

"Well, my day is definitely ruined, but thank you. I would rather this one day be ruined than the rest of my life." She sighed.

"Glad we're on the same page."

She put her hand up to her forehead to use it to shield her vision from the sun as she focused in on Kyle. "What are you doing here anyway? You do know that you're supposed to be at the United Center warming up for the game, right?"

"Yeah." He smirked.

"Oh, so I guess you don't care about getting fined or fired, hunh?"

"Yeah, but I thought letting you know the truth was more important than any amount of money I will have to pay if I get fined or lose if I get fired." Kyle looked off and shoved his hands into the pockets of his warm-up jogging pants.

Karen squinted, gazing at his strong jawline. "Thank you."

Kyle towered over her as he shifted to stand directly in front of her to mask her from the sun.

"Can I ask you something?" Kyle stared into her eyes.

She lowered her head and twiddled her fingers. "Sure."

"Did you love him at all?"

She looked up at him briefly, saw the intensity in his eyes, but then lowered them to focus on the beading on her dress. She spoke softly. "Not in my heart. I knew he wasn't the one for me, but like I said in there, I'm just at a point in my life where I want love. I want to be married and have kids. I was willing to do that with him."

"Even though you knew it wasn't real love?"

"Hey, don't judge me." She looked up at him.

"So, I know you might think this is none of my business, but are you going to wait for true love or marry the next most presentable guy you meet?"

"Lesson learned. I'm going to keep my impatient tail busy with my career and wait until I meet the right one. I'll know in my heart and not just with my thoughts that he is the right one." Karen laughed.

"What are you laughing at?"

"Oh, nothing. Melanie asked me a few times if I knew the difference between loving someone and being in love with him. I never answered her, but in my heart I knew the answer."

"So, have you ever been in love with someone?"

Karen paused. "Yes." She lowered her head and traced the patterns of beads on her dress.

"So, if you were really in love before, why didn't it work out?"

"Life, pride got in the way. Or maybe it just wasn't the right timing for him and me. I don't know." She kept her head down.

Kyle inched closer to her. "Do you think if he came back around you would be willing to give him another chance?"

"I don't know, maybe."

He drew closer to her and lifted her chin to lock eyes with her.

"So, do you think that you'd be willing to give this person that you were once in love with another chance if he told you how sorry he was for the things he did in his past, way before he met you?"

"I don't know, maybe." Karen bit her lip as she stared into his eyes.

Kyle inched even closer to her. "Karen?"

"Hunh?" Her already parted lips were dry.

"Karen, do you think that you could give me another chance?"

"I have a question for you."

"Ask it. I swear to tell the truth, the whole truth, and nothing but the truth so help me God." Kyle held his right hand up.

Karen laughed. "You can put your hand down. This is not a courtroom." She paused, wondering if she should ask him the question that gnawed at her heart and mind ever since Melanie had shared the information with her.

"Karen, don't be shy. Just ask me."

"Okay. Did you really turn down twenty million dollars from the Clippers just to come to Chicago to be with me?"

"That Andrew talks too much." Kyle laughed. He stepped closer to her. "Yes, you were the deciding factor for me signing with the Bulls. If you were in Chicago, I wanted to be here."

The silence between them was deafening to Karen. She searched for something else to say to him, but his answer to her question was still tap dancing on her emotions.

"Now will you answer my question?"

"Kyle, we can talk after the game, but judging by the sun beginning to set, I think that you should get over to the United Center. I need to get over there as well and get mic'd up."

Kyle shook his head. He had forgotten for a second that he had a game to play in that night. "You're right, I do need to get over there, but there are some things I just have to know before I go."

Karen tilted her head to the side looking up at him. "Like what?"

"Like why you're scheduled to cover a game the same day of your wedding and—"

"Before you ask your other question, let me answer the first one."

He nodded his head.

"Because my career is very important to me. Me covering the championship game tonight is huge for my broadcasting future. I had a man that understood that."

Kyle jerked his head back in laughter. "Glad you used the word 'had'. A thing of the past."

"Whatever. Hurry up and ask me your other question so that we can get over to the stadium."

Kyle inched even closer to Karen to where she could feel the warmth of his breath mingling in with the warmth of the setting sun on her skin. She shuddered.

"I asked you already." He traced a part of her hairline before smoothing her hair back. "Would you be willing to give the guy you were really in love with another chance?" His stare into her eyes never wavered.

"I'll think about it." Karen smirked.

"Oh my god, woman. You drive me insane, but I love it." He stared into her eyes placing his hands on the small of her back. He tilted his head and lowered it just close enough to brush her lips with his.

She willed herself to speak. "Kyle, maybe we shouldn't do this right now."

"You're right. Maybe not, but who cares." He gave her a quick but passionate peck on her lips and then smiled, looking into her eyes. "You know where I have to go now, but breakfast tomorrow?"

"Yes." The warmth of her smile matched that of the suns.

He turned to head to his car and she patted him on the butt as he jogged off. He looked back, winking at her. He ran faster to his car fueled by the thought of them being together again and the hope that he would get back to the stadium on time.

Dennis stood on the church's stairs the entire time Karen and Kyle spoke to one another. He stayed back, knowing that he was no match for Kyle. He had tried running after Karen right when she first stormed out of the church, but Kyle stopped him and choked him so that he still felt the bruises on his lungs. He knew to keep his distance from Kyle.

Karen smiled, unaware that Dennis was nearby. She reached into her purse and grabbed her key fob, hit the button to disarm the alarm, and then jumped in her car.

She exhaled a happy breath and put her car into drive. Her foot was on the gas when Dennis jumped in front of it.

"Dennis, move out the way," she screamed.

"Karen, I'm sorry for what I did. I know it was stupid of me and I made a mistake. I just wanted him out of the way so that you and I could be together. Everything I did was because I love you, baby, and I always have. It's our wedding day. Won't you just come back in and we get married? We can work this out, I promise. Karen, I won't do anything else to hurt you. I love you. We're meant to be."

"Dennis, I suggest you move out of the way."

Dennis remained in front of the car pleading for Karen to get out and talk to him.

She shook her head from side to side as she tapped the gas pedal inching closer to Dennis.

"Karen? Karen? Can you just get out of the car and talk to me?"

She stuck her head out of the driver's side window so that she could be clearly heard. "Dennis, I suggest you get out from in front of the car on your own before it moves you out of the way."

He refused to move thinking Karen didn't have the heart to hit him with the car.

He was wrong.

Other Books Available

Sisterhood Chronicles Series
Underneath It All
Discovery
Untold
When It Happens To You
All Things Considered

Forever Friends Series
Catch Me If You Can
It's Complicated

Limelight Series
Hues
Tones
Vision

Standalone Titles
After All Is Said & Done
The Bid Catcher: Distinguished Gentlemen Series

*(Best if you read Forever Friends series before
reading Sisterhood Chronicles 3)*

COMING SOON

The Kissing Game: Love Alive 1

ABOUT THE AUTHOR

Anita Davis is a former elementary teacher born and raised in Chicago. Although she wrote short stories much of her childhood, she didn't unlock and cultivate her passion as a writer until she became a writing teacher for middle school students. The more she had to create sample writings for her students, the more she realized her passion and ability to tell stories in the written form. She decided to hone her craft as a writer by completing her Master of Fine Arts in Creative Writing via National University. She now pursues writing books most of her time, in addition to being a flight attendant. Anita seeks to encourage, engage, and entertain her readers.

She is Co-Founder of Book Euphoria, a group of Chicago authors bound by their love of literature. Book Euphoria hosts literary events and they also founded the empowerment movement, Black Girl Passion.

Anita writes contemporary romantic women's fiction and seeks to encourage, engage, and entertain her readers.

authoranitadavis@gmail.com
www.authoranitadavis.com
Facebook: Anita Davis and Author page: Author Anita Davis
Instagram: @authoranitadavis   Twitter: @_AnitaDavis

www.ingramcontent.com/pod-product-compliance
Lightning Source LLC
Chambersburg PA
CBHW062135170626
46813CB00002B/709